THE FORTUNES OF TEXAS

Follow the lives and loves of a complex family with a rich history and deep ties in the Lone Star State.

THE WEDDING GIFT

The town of Rambling Rose, Texas, is brimming with excitement over the upcoming wedding of five Fortune couples! They're scheduled to tie the knot on New Year's Eve, but one wedding gift arrives early, setting off a mystery that could send shock waves through the entire Fortune family...

Josh Fortune has a reputation—he falls in love at the drop of a hat, but it never lasts. He's determined to apply the brakes when he meets Kirby Harris, a young widowed mother of two, who makes the best coffee in town. But he must fight to prove to everyone—even his own family!—that he can be the forever kind of man she and her little girls need...

Dear Reader,

I love single-parent romances. There's something so real about watching a parent navigate the dating world while raising children. In *A Fortune in the Family*, widowed mom of two adorable girls Kirby Harris gets a second chance at love. After her husband's death, she convinced herself that there was no place for a man in her life. That is, until she meets Josh Fortune.

Josh Fortune believes in love. He wants to be in a committed relationship that will lead to a future filled with love, laughter and children. Unfortunately, he's heard the dreaded *it's not you, it's me* speech over and over.

When he lays eyes on Kirby, he falls. Hard. She tries to slot him into the friend zone, but he's not having it. He's determined to show Kirby that she can love again.

It was so much fun watching as Josh and Kirby's friendship blossomed into a love that can last a lifetime. I hope you enjoy reading it as much as I enjoyed writing it.

I love hearing from my readers, so feel free to stop by my website, kathydouglassbooks.com, and drop me a message. While you're there, sign up for my monthly newsletter.

Happy reading!

Kathy

A Fortune in the Family

KATHY DOUGLASS

Special thanks and acknowledgment are given to Kathy Douglass for her contribution to The Fortunes of Texas: The Wedding Gift miniseries.

ISBN-13: 978-1-335-40852-5

A Fortune in the Family

For questions and comments about the quality of this book, please contact us at CustomerService@Harlequin.com.

Harlequin Enterprises ULC
22 Adelaide St. West, 41st Floor
Toronto, Ontario M5H 4E3, Canada
www.Harlequin.com

Printed in U.S.A.

Kathy Douglass came by her love of reading naturally—both of her parents were readers. She would finish one book and pick up another. Then she attended law school and traded romances for legal opinions.

After the birth of her two children, her love of reading turned into a love of writing. Kathy now spends her days writing the small-town contemporary novels she enjoys reading.

Books by Kathy Douglass

Harlequin Special Edition

Sweet Briar Sweethearts

How to Steal the Lawman's Heart
The Waitress's Secret
The Rancher and the City Girl
Winning Charlotte Back
The Rancher's Return
A Baby Between Friends
The Single Mom's Second Chance
The Soldier Under Her Tree
Redemption on Rivers Ranch

Furever Yours

The City Girl's Homecoming

Montana Mavericks: What Happened to Beatrix?

The Maverick's Baby Arrangement

Visit the Author Profile page
at Harlequin.com for more titles.

This book is dedicated to all of the bloggers, reviewers and podcasters who have supported me in my career. There are too many of you to name, but I am grateful to each and every one of you.

This book is also dedicated with love to my husband and sons, who support me in everything that I do. I love you more than words can say.

Chapter One

Josh Fortune leaned against his quartz kitchen counter, swallowed the last of the stale doughnuts from the box he'd picked up who knows when, and chased it down with a passable cup of coffee. The rain pounded on the windows, and he mentally reviewed the jobs on the various work sites where he was the contractor. Rambling Rose, Texas, a town between Houston and Austin, had become a hot location in recent years and people were snapping up properties as soon as they came on the market. As a carpenter and the owner of his own contracting business, he had several renovating projects going at any given time.

His cousins owned Fortune Brothers Construction, where two of his brothers worked. Although he'd considered joining them, he'd eventually decided to stay on his own. Perhaps it stemmed from being the youngest brother who'd been bossed about by his brothers growing up, but he liked being his own boss. His family understood and had recommended him for jobs that were too small for their business.

His phone buzzed and he read the Caller ID onscreen before he answered it.

"What's up, Kane?" he said to his brother.

"I'm wondering if you could do me a favor."

"Do you even have to ask? Just name it." Gary Fortune's kids might not have been raised with as much money as their recently discovered affluent Texas or Florida or New Orleans cousins, but they had managed to live just as richly in their own ways.

"Well, the favor isn't for me. It's actually for someone I know."

"Okay," Josh said. He put the phone on speaker so he could wash his empty mug while he talked. "What does this friend need?"

"Have you ever been to Kirby's Perks?"

"I can't say that I have. What does that have to do with anything?"

"I was there this morning to grab a cup of coffee before work and the roof is leaking. I was hoping you could stop by and help her out. That is, if you have the time."

"I have time. Text me her address and I'll head over now."

"Thanks. I owe you."

"We're brothers. You don't owe me a thing."

Josh hung up and his phone pinged immediately. He read the address while walking out the back door. When the rain hit him, he dashed across the yard to his shed. He grabbed two boxes of shingles and roofing nails that were left over from a previous job and tossed them into the truck bed. After hooking his extension ladder onto his work truck, he drove off.

He had only lived in Rambling Rose for a couple of months and had spent that time getting his new business established and finding a house to rent, so he hadn't had the opportunity to visit Kirby's coffee shop before. As he pulled into the parking lot beside the gaily painted building and hopped out of his truck, he wondered why that was. But now wasn't the time to stand around thinking. He was getting soaked, and no doubt Kirby was waiting expectantly for his help.

He dashed the short distance to the glass front door. The sign—Kirby's Perks—was written in purple curvy letters above a coffee cup with pink, yellow and purple flowers on the front. The logo was appealing, and he felt welcome just looking at it.

He stepped inside and glanced around, observing several things at once. First, there were buckets and pans on several tables and even more on the floor, catching water dripping from the ceiling. A few of them were near to overflowing. They were located on one side of the room, so more than likely the problem was isolated to one section of the roof. Second, there was a good deal of people sitting at tables in the dry part of the room, clearly unbothered by the water falling only feet away. But the thing he noticed most was the appetizing aroma. Josh inhaled and got a whiff of coffee that smelled much better than the stuff he made at home. He wondered if it would taste as good as it smelled.

Dodging raindrops and sidestepping buckets, Josh headed toward the front of the shop. A sheet of plastic was draped across the top of a display case housing a wide variety of doughnuts, flaky croissants and other pastries.

A woman dressed in a purple T-shirt and an apron with the Kirby's Perks logo on it came over to him. Despite the fact that she had to be frustrated, she smiled at him.

"How can I help you?" Her voice was low and just as sexy as her body.

"Actually, I'm here to help you. I'm Josh Fortune. My brother Kane called me about your roof."

"Oh, thank you so much for coming so quickly,"

she said, clasping her hands together in front of her. "I appreciate any help you can give me."

"No worries. I have my ladder, so I'll just go check out the roof and see what the problem is." He smothered a groan. What an inane thing to say. He removed his cap, determined to start over. A drop of water plopped on his head and instinctively he looked up. Another drop fell right on his forehead and ran into his eye. He blinked it away. "That didn't come out right. I have a pretty good idea what the problem is. I'll just take a look and see how bad it is. Fingers crossed it's something I can fix today and nothing that requires replacing the roof."

She held up her hands, her slender fingers crossed.

Their luck held. A quick investigation revealed a roof that was old but generally in good condition for its age. A patch job would suffice for now.

Descending the ladder, he felt eager to step inside. He told himself it was because he wanted to relieve Kirby's mind and not because he wanted another look at her. With clear brown skin, deep, dark brown eyes, full lips and high cheekbones, the woman was unquestionably gorgeous.

And that body. Although she was wearing an apron over her jeans and T-shirt, it did little to hide her sexy curves.

Reminding himself that he was here to work, he stepped into the coffee shop. He glanced around and saw Kirby placing an empty bucket beneath a stream of water. She sighed and placed her hands on her hips. For a second she appeared defeated. But then she rallied, straightening her shoulders and lifting her chin. Good. She had spunk. He liked that.

"I've got good news," he said, approaching her.

"Don't hold back," she said. "Shout it out. I could use all the good news I can get."

"You don't need a new roof. At least not yet. And I have the material I need to patch your roof inside my truck. It shouldn't take me long to get it done."

"Thank you."

"You're welcome. I'll get right to it."

She nodded and he turned to go. As he left, he would swear he could feel her watching him walk away. Smiling, he stepped back outside and into the torrential downpour. Suddenly he wasn't bothered by the weather. Quite the opposite. Now he was grateful for the rain, leaky roofs and brothers who asked for favors.

Kirby watched as Josh Fortune walked back into the storm. Even though there was no place in her life for a man—she was a single mother with two little girls to raise and a business to run—she couldn't help but notice how attractive he was. Which was completely out of character for her. She hadn't given a man a first look, much less a second, since her beloved Will was taken from her. Although she no longer felt the breath-stealing sorrow at the thought of her late husband, she still experienced a pang in her heart, and she closed her eyes as she waited for it to pass.

She and Will had known each other all of their lives. They'd been friends as kids, and later high school sweethearts. They'd dated all through college and married right after graduation. Theirs had been a wedding of a lifetime, one she and Will had planned on talking about on their fiftieth anniversary.

But that was before Will had been diagnosed with an aggressive form of liver cancer. He'd died three years ago, before they'd even had the opportunity to celebrate their tenth anniversary.

When Will had discovered that he was sick, he made her promise to keep the coffee shop going. It had been her dream for ages, and they'd worked together to make it happen. Her business had thrived and now she had many faithful customers, like the ones currently going about their day as if it wasn't raining inside nearly as hard as it was outside. And so, despite the fact that the building was fighting against her today, Kirby's Perks was open for business.

She glanced around, grateful for each of her patrons. They were as eclectic as they were loyal. Rebecca, the quirky, redheaded fiction writer in her fifties, was downing her third cup of coffee of the morning. She swore she couldn't function if she didn't have at least four cups of Kirby's coffee in her system. She claimed she did her best writing in the coffee shop and that she'd never meet her deadlines if not for Kirby. Rebecca had even dedicated her last book to her. Right now she was doodling on a pad and pretending not to eavesdrop on another customer's phone conversation. No doubt some piece of it would find its way into her next book, which was why Kirby always started each conversation with Rebecca by saying it was off the record.

Annette, Kirby's former barista who was now a college student at a local university was talking to Justine, a new mother of a sweet baby boy named Morgan. Martin, an eighty-plus man with a grizzled beard, was nursing his coffee. He was a kind fellow who generally conversed with whomever happened to sit near him and had no shortage of opinions on just about everything. He and Kirby talked for a few minutes each day and she loved to hear stories of his youth. Of course, the rain had pushed him away from his normal table near the counter, but he seemed just as happy today to read the newspaper he'd brought in with him.

The bell over the door jingled and Kirby pulled herself out of her musings to fix a cinnamon latte for a customer. She'd worried that the storm would slow business but she'd been wrong. Too bad that luck hadn't extended to the roof.

As she emptied buckets and filled coffee cups, she tried not to think about just how much the roof repair would set her back. The constant pounding wasn't a good sign and she was starting to believe the problem was more extensive than Josh had let on. Maybe what he considered good news was catastrophic to her. Whenever the noise stopped, she would look up expecting to see him walk in and tell her his initial assessment had been wrong. And each time she caught a glimpse of him as he went up and down the ladder, she couldn't help staring. She might not be in the market for a man, but that didn't keep her from appreciating how good-looking he was.

His blond hair was sun-streaked and his skin was tanned as if he spent hours working outdoors. His broad back, well-defined biceps and shoulders were those of a man who was no stranger to physical work. Her cheeks warmed as she recalled how nice his muscular thighs and backside had looked in those faded jeans. He was definitely one perfect specimen of a man.

Perfect for some other woman.

A woman whose hands weren't filled running a business and raising a kindergartner and second grader. Her little girls needed all of her love and attention right now and would for the foreseeable future. She didn't have time or energy to spare. She had nothing to offer a man—even one as appealing as Josh Fortune.

Finally the hammering stopped. The water coming from the ceiling, which had gone from a steady stream to a trickle as Josh worked, now became an occasional drip. She was probably the only person in the country who wasn't caught up in the renovation television show craze, but even she knew that all of the water that had come through the roof couldn't have possibly dripped onto the floor. Some of it had to be pooled in the ceiling. Just how much was the question.

Maybe Josh would know. And if the stars aligned just right, it wouldn't cost much to get everything taken care of. At moments like this, rare though they were, she wished she hadn't made that promise to Will to keep this place going. It hadn't been easy with two little girls. But no matter how difficult it had been at times, the business had been her saving grace. It had given her something to do and somewhere to go when she would have preferred to hold her daughters in her arms and just cry over all they'd lost.

But wallowing in misery would have been unfair to Violet and Lily. Violet had been four when Will died, and old enough to miss him. Kirby's heart had broken over and over again as she'd watch her little girl stand in the front window every evening, waiting for her daddy to come home from work. Kirby had explained that daddy was in heaven, but Violet hadn't understood what that meant. Will had traveled occasionally for work, and each time he'd come home. Violet hadn't understood why his going to heaven would keep him from coming back.

Lily had only been two when Will died. At first she asked about him, but it hadn't taken long for her to accept his absence and get on with her life. That had been even more painful to Kirby than Violet's tears.

It broke Kirby's heart to know that Lily didn't have any memories of her father and that Violet had very few. Kirby did all she could to keep Will's memory alive, telling stories about him and placing family photographs beside each of the girls' beds, but there was only so much she could do. She knew the beautiful, happy past they'd shared was gone and the wonderful future they'd planned would never come to be. It was in all of their best interests for them to soldier on and live in the present. For Kirby, that present didn't include a man. Truth be told, there wouldn't be a man in her future, either. She'd loved Will with all of her heart and soul. He'd been a special man. And special men were rare.

Yet she hadn't been able to stop looking out the window at Josh Fortune whenever he came into view.

Kirby was pouring Rebecca's fourth cup of coffee when her cell phone rang. One look at the number made her heart pound with anxiety. It was the school her girls attended. She wasn't able to rid herself of the dread that accompanied every one of the school's phone calls. Losing Will had taught her to expect the worst.

Answering the phone, she headed for the kitchen where she would have privacy.

"Mrs. Harris, this is Deadra Hawkins."

Kirby recognized the school secretary's voice. Mrs. Hawkins was a kindly grandmother whom students and parents alike adored. She had a way of making even the worst news palatable.

"Is something wrong?" Kirby asked, hoping the other woman was calling to request pastries for an upcoming school event.

"Nothing major," she said calmly. "Lily isn't feeling well, and she needs to get picked up."

"I see." Lily had seemed fine when Kirby dropped her off at school a couple of hours ago. Perhaps she'd picked up a bug. Little kids were more willing to share germs than they were crayons. "I'm on my way."

"Drive carefully. She's lying down in the nurse's office and she'll be fine until you get here."

Kirby ended the phone call, grabbed her purse from her office and returned to the front of the coffee shop. Rebecca had booted up her laptop and was typing rapidly, clearly on a roll. Annette had already left, and Martin was talking with Justine, who was feeding Morgan. Kirby hated the idea of kicking them out, especially in this deluge, but she didn't have a choice. Hillary, her barista, had called in sick and Kirby was alone. She needed to close the coffee shop while she picked up her child. And depending on how sick Lily was, Kirby might need to keep the shop closed for the rest of the day while she nursed Lily at home.

Ordinarily she could call on her mother or mother-in-law for assistance, but they were both out of town today. Her parents were in the Bahamas and Will's were in Austin, where their daughter was expecting her first child any day.

"I'm all finished," Josh said, pulling her away from her musings. She blinked and stared at him. Rain dripped from his navy slicker, which he'd left unbuttoned, yet he somehow looked sexy. His blond hair was plastered against his head. His navy T-shirt with white letters advertising Josh Fortune Carpentry clung to his muscular torso. Even his jeans were wet. Despite the fact that Kirby knew he had to be uncomfortable and was no doubt longing to get out of his wet clothes and take a hot shower, he was smiling. And that smile warmed her heart, and for a moment all of her troubles vanished.

"Thank you for your help. If you would write up a bill for me, I'll write you a check." She pulled a checkbook from her purse. "I hate to rush you, but I need to close the shop for a bit. My daughter is sick and I have to pick her up from school."

"Why do you have to close?"

She obviously hadn't been as clear as she'd thought. She stepped behind the counter and turned off the coffeepot. "Because I need to leave. My employee called in sick today and there's nobody to take care of business while I'm gone."

"I'll do it."

"You'll do what?"

"I'll handle the shop until you get back."

"Why would you do that?"

"Because you need the help." He said it simply, as if his reason was obvious.

"I sell more than just coffee. Do you know how to make a latte? Cappuccino?"

"Are the recipes written down anywhere?"

"Yes. I have them taped to the back of the countertop."

"I can read so I should be all right."

"I don't know." She couldn't keep the skepticism from her voice.

He shrugged. "What's to know? You need help and I don't mind helping. Besides, do you really want to ask your customers to leave? They all look so comfortable. You wouldn't want to send that sweet baby or that old man into that downpour, would you?"

"Of course not. But I can't ask you to do this, either."

"You didn't ask. I volunteered. There's a difference."

"I still don't understand why."

"Because I'm a nice guy." He held up a hand as if to forestall any other argument she might have. "You'd better go. Your little girl is waiting."

She imagined Lily lying there on the nurse's cot, wondering why it was taking her mommy so long to come and get her. "I won't be long."

"Take your time. I've got things handled here." Josh stepped around the counter and without missing a beat, he grabbed an apron off the hook on the wall, pulled it over his head and tied it behind his back in one smooth motion. "I need to look official," he said, flashing her a grin.

"Sure." She grabbed the umbrella she kept by the door and darted for her car. As she guided the SUV down the road, thoughts of Josh danced through her mind. He was so easygoing. Happy-go-lucky. As if nothing bothered him. But then, he probably didn't have the responsibilities she did.

When Kirby reached the school, she headed to the office. Mrs. Hawkins smiled at her. "Don't look so worried. Lily is fine. Just a little stomachache."

Kirby blew out a breath. Lily was a sweetheart who loved school, but lately she didn't seem to enjoy it as much. Kirby had believed all-day kindergarten was a godsend, but maybe it was too much for her daughter. At first Lily had loved every minute of school. She'd even been ready to go bright and early on Saturday mornings. Now she was frequently reluctant in the mornings, dragging her feet until they were nearly late. Was there something going on that was upsetting her? Lily, who always told Kirby everything, hadn't mentioned a problem. And the kindergarten teacher, Mrs. Bennett, hadn't brought anything to Kirby's attention.

Kirby signed out Lily for the day. A minute later the nurse arrived with Lily beside her.

"Her assignments are in her backpack," the nurse said.

"Thank you. I'll make sure she does them."

Kirby held Lily's hand as they walked down the hall. When they reached the door, she picked Lily up in one arm and held the umbrella in the other hand as she speed-walked to the car. Once they were inside the car, Lily flashed her a bright smile as if she felt just fine.

"Feeling better?"

"Yep. Can we listen to my music?"

Little rascal. Although Kirby was glad that Lily's

"stomachache" had vanished, she wished she knew what was bothering Lily.

Kirby turned on a kids' music DVD and instantly Lily was singing about sticky bubblegum. After two songs, Kirby paused the music. "How was school today?"

Lily shrugged.

"Did something happen?"

"Like what?"

Kirby sighed. So much for the indirect route. If you wanted an answer from Lily, you had to ask direct questions. The problem was, Kirby wasn't sure what she should ask. "Is there someone who isn't your friend?"

"Mrs. Bennett says that we're all friends."

"That's right. But sometimes friends can hurt your feelings without meaning to. When that happens it's okay to tell me or Mrs. Bennett."

"Okay. Can I listen to my songs again?"

Sighing, Kirby turned the music back up and continued down the road.

When they got to the coffee shop, they made a mad dash to the front door, Lily giggling the whole time as if she were at recess.

"That was fun," she said the moment they were inside.

"I'm glad you enjoyed it," Kirby said. "Now, take

off your backpack. Then we can find a table and you can start your schoolwork."

"Okay, Mommy. I like coming to work with you."

"I know." Violet and Lily had spent a lot of time here. They'd practically grown up in the shop and loved coming to work with Mommy. It was their home away from home.

Kirby kept dolls, puzzles, board games, crayons and coloring books here for the girls. Even though they enjoyed playing with their toys, they delighted in being able to help her. She'd had aprons and T-shirts with the Kirby's Perks logos made for them, and they loved wearing them as they followed her around the shop.

"Who's that?" Lily asked, pointing to the counter.

Kirby turned and saw Josh making a cappuccino. Or rather, attempting one. He stood there pushing buttons on the machine and scratching his head. There were several cups stacked beside him, proof of previous failures. The machine was obviously getting the best of him.

"Who is he, Mommy?" Lily repeated, tapping Kirby on her side.

"That's my friend."

"He doesn't know what he's doing."

Kirby laughed. "I know. I think I'll go and help him."

After getting Lily settled at a table, she hurried

behind the counter. The customer, a man with either extreme patience, a good sense of humor or all the time in the world, gave Josh suggestions on how to work the cappuccino machine.

"Oh, no. Don't try that, either," Kirby said, rushing over to Josh. "That won't work."

Josh shrugged and gave her a smile. Did nothing fluster the man? He stepped aside and began untying the strings of the apron. "This has to be the most complicated machine ever created. My new buddy, Dan, and I have been trying to figure it out for at least ten minutes."

Kirby smiled at Josh and then at Dan. "I'll have a cappuccino for each of you in no time flat. And, Dan, in appreciation for your patience, it's on the house."

"That's not necessary," Dan replied. "Watching Josh has been entertaining to say the least. But I appreciate the offer."

Kirby washed her hands and then stepped up to the machine.

"I think you're going to need this," Josh said, pulling the apron over his head. Kirby held out her hand to take it from him, but before she knew what he intended, he'd dropped it over her head. In the blink of an eye, he was behind her, securing the apron around her waist. His hands brushed against the small of her back, sending goose bumps from the point of contact throughout her body.

"Thank you," she murmured. Somehow she managed to keep her voice from trembling. "I'll get those cappuccinos for you."

She quickly made one for her customer, refusing his payment since he'd had to wait for so long. He thanked her and promised to come back again with his wife.

"You're both welcome at any time," Kirby said, handing over his beverage.

"And let me get yours," she said to Josh. At that moment, the door opened, and three more customers stepped inside.

"Take care of them first," Josh said. "I don't mind waiting."

Kirby nodded, trying not to stare as he walked over to a table. For the most part his clothes were no longer wet, but his T-shirt still clung to his torso, emphasizing his muscular physique.

Telling herself not to gawk, Kirby turned her attention to her customers. After she'd filled their orders, she glanced around, looking for Josh. Lily had left her table and was now sitting across from him. Kirby prepared Josh's cappuccino and carried it over to him.

As she approached the table, she heard Lily's voice. She was telling Josh one of the fanciful tales she tended to make up. From the time she could string enough words together to form a sentence, she had been creating stories in worlds where animals and plants talked to each other. Her tales also included little children who possessed a variety of marvelous abilities, depending on which skill was necessary to advance the plot.

"What did the fairy princess do next?" Josh asked. His voice contained just the right amount of interest, but Kirby imagined he was simply being polite. No doubt he was hoping she would rescue him so that he could get on with his day.

"She picked up the ladybug and took her home to her mommy and daddy. And everyone lived happily ever after."

"That's good. And a very nice story."

"I know lots of stories," Lily said, taking a deep breath.

"And I'll listen to them tonight," Kirby interrupted before her daughter could launch into another one. She set Josh's cup on the table. "But right now, you have schoolwork to finish. And Mr. Fortune has places to go and things to do."

"No, I don't," Josh said. "I'm enjoying Lily's stories. She has quite the imagination."

"Who's Mr. Fortune?" Lily asked.

"He is."

"His name is Josh. He's my friend now, too."

Josh's eyes filled with concern. "I hope you don't mind that I said she could call me Josh."

Kirby generally preferred for her kids to address adults by their last names, or at least hang a title on the first name, but since she doubted Lily would see Josh again after today, she didn't see the harm.

"It's fine. But you don't have to entertain Lily."

"Actually, it's the other way around. She's entertaining me."

He sounded so sincere she knew he was telling her the truth and she smiled. Although the male members in her family tried to be there for her girls, they could only do so much. Her father and father-in-law were getting up there in age. They were great at telling stories and playing board games, but neither of them could run around with the girls for hours on end like their father had done. Kirby's brother tried to attend the girls' dance recitals, but he lived in Houston. Besides, he had a family of his own and his own kids' activities to attend. The way Lily eagerly lapped up Josh's attention brought home how much her girls missed by not having their father in their lives. But Will was gone and no one could ever replace him. He'd been a one-of-a-kind father. A one-of-a-kind husband. *A one-of-a-kind man.* Kirby was just going to have to be both mom and dad.

Be that as it may, it did please her to see the way Josh treated her little girl.

The bell over the door jangled and a large group

stepped inside. "All right. But feel free to excuse yourself when you've heard enough stories."

Josh nodded and took a sip of his drink. "Delicious."

"It helps when you know how to work the machine," Kirby quipped as she walked away. Even without looking she knew Josh's eyes were following her, so she added a little more swing to her hips. When she realized what she was doing, she froze. Why was she flirting with him? There wasn't room for a man in her life. She barely had time to breathe. Besides, she didn't *want* a man in her life.

But why was she suddenly not as sure about that as she'd once been?

Chapter Two

Josh watched as Kirby walked away, his eyes drawn to her perfectly shaped bottom, and then turned his attention back to her adorable daughter. He wasn't simply being polite when he'd said that Lily had been entertaining him. The little girl was positively delightful.

When he'd first moved to Rambling Rose, he'd stayed with his brother Brady, a father to five-year-old twin boys. Tyler and Toby were way more rambunctious than Lily but being around her made him think of his nephews. He made a mental note to get together with his brother soon so he could roughhouse with his nephews.

The stories Lily shared were clever and revealed a creative mind as well as a kind spirit. In each story she told, someone willingly helped someone in need. There were happy families filled with great affection for each other. Clearly she was being raised with much love.

Kirby's laughter floated over to him and he glanced in her direction. She was smiling as she handed over a pastry to a customer. Was there a man in her life? She didn't wear a wedding ring, but that could be because she had to wash her hands often while working. Rings might be an annoyance.

After Kirby served the last of the customers, she returned to the table he and Lily were sharing. She sat beside her daughter and kissed her on the forehead. "How's that schoolwork coming?"

Lily held up a colorful math paper. The numbers scrawled there were of varying sizes, but from a quick glance Josh could see that she'd answered each of the questions correctly. Given the fact that she'd been talking to him a good deal of the time and splitting her attention, that was quite impressive.

"And your spelling?"

Lily sighed and rested her chin on her fist. "I'm not finished yet."

"Let's work on that, shall we?"

Lily nodded and picked up her pencil.

"I don't think I thanked you for getting this place back in order," Kirby said to Josh.

"You don't have to thank me." While she'd been gone, he'd taken up the plastic off the counters, dried the tables and chairs, and mopped up the few puddles that remained. It hadn't taken long and he'd been much more adept at doing that than he'd been at making fancy drinks. But then, the physical work was in his skill set.

"Of course I do. And thank you again for coming to my aid earlier today. Now, how much do I owe you for your work?"

"This delicious cup of coffee should cover it."

Her eyebrows raised and she shook her head, sending her lovely hair cascading around her shoulders. "You can't be serious. I saw you carrying shingles up the ladder and I know those aren't cheap. More than that, you spent a lot of time on my roof. Time that you could have spent doing other work and getting paid for it."

"Don't worry about it. I'm not. I didn't use that many shingles. Besides, they were some I had left over from a job. They were just sitting around my shed and taking up space. And as far as time goes, I work for myself and for the most part I set my own schedule."

"What do you do? Kane didn't say."

"What did my brother say about me?"

"Not much. When he stopped in this morning and saw the water pouring in, he said that he had a brother who could help."

"Oh. I'm a carpenter and I own a contracting business."

She laughed softly, a merry sound, and he enjoyed it. "You must be busy, then."

"Busy enough," he replied. "All the gentrification going on in Rambling Rose is good for business. But sometimes I like to take off my contractor hat and do some of the actual carpentry. Lately I haven't had the chance to pick up a hammer and do some real work in weeks. So when you think about it, you did me a favor."

"Right." She drew the word out over a few syllables. It sounded as if she were purring and he wondered what it would take to make her purr in his arms. He shot down the thought before it could get the better of him. The last thing he needed to do was start imagining making love with a woman he barely knew. Especially while he was seated across the table from her young daughter.

And weren't his siblings always teasing him about his tendency to fall in love at the drop of a hat? Weren't they always warning him against putting everything into the relationship while he and the woman were still in the get-to-know-you stage? He'd always been the one eager to get serious while the women hadn't been. He couldn't count the number of times he'd been the recipient of the "it's not you it's me" speech. The last time had been especially painful and was part of the catalyst for him moving from upstate New York to Rambling Rose where he hoped to have better luck dating. Yet here he was again, getting ahead of himself without knowing much about Kirby. They hadn't even reached the get-to-know-you stage. If he wasn't careful, he'd be head over heels in love with her simply because she had a gorgeous smile, beautiful brown skin, a sexy body and a sweet personality. Besides, for all he knew, she was involved with someone. Or married.

Nope. He needed to get away so he could clear his head.

"I'm done," Lily said, waving her worksheet in the air and saving him the need to reply.

"And on that note, I'd better get a move on. There are a couple of things I need to do before the day is out. But I'll be back in a little while to check on the roof."

"Thank you. I appreciate all you've done for me."

"It was my pleasure."

"Bye, Josh," Lily said, giving him a big smile.

"See you later, Lily."

Josh hopped into his pickup truck and then glanced at himself in the rearview mirror. He groaned. His hair had dried but now it was sticking out on end and going every which way. There was a bit of dirt smeared across his forehead and more was dotted across his face. He looked like a dog who'd played in a mud puddle. It was a wonder that Kirby hadn't laughed every time she glanced at him. He was definitely going to have to shower before he went back to the coffee shop. Obviously he couldn't make another first impression, but his second impression was going to be a major improvement.

He hadn't been exaggerating when he told Kirby that he was very busy. Rambling Rose was a town midway between Austin and Houston. Until about ten years ago, it was a forgotten blue-collar town. After it was featured in an indie documentary, out-of-towners—including his cousin, Callum Fortune—began flocking in and buying up property, gentrifying everything they could get their hands on. That led to a lot of work that had as yet to slow. As a result, he had been busy since he'd come to town, especially with the help of his cousins at Fortune Brothers Construction and their referrals. He made a point to check on his work sites at least twice a week, more if several trades were going to be on-site at once. A good deal of his job involved trouble-shooting. If he could keep problems and conflicts to a minimum, everyone was happy, and the work got done more quickly.

He pulled onto a street where a crew was renovating a large old house. The new owner wanted to knock down so many walls and rearrange so many rooms that Josh thought it would have made more sense to buy a house that better suited the owner's style. There was nothing special about the lot that he could see that would make the site preferable to any other. But then, he was only the contractor. The owner and the designer were in charge of the aesthetics. Now that the engineer had approved the plans, Josh's job was to make sure that everything was done as requested and on schedule.

"How's it going?" he called to Eddie, his friend and the plumber on this project. They'd been friends and had worked on a lot of jobs together in New York. Eddie had just gotten divorced when Josh decided to move to Rambling Rose. Eddie had wanted a fresh start and had recently relocated.

"A-OK. Of course, we'd be moving along more quickly if the owners didn't keep showing up unannounced every day to take a look at the progress. They insist on asking everyone questions and slowing them down. I don't even need to tell you that they were wearing shorts and flip-flops again."

Josh blew out a breath. "I'll talk to them again and let them know that this is a work site and that it can be dangerous. Those home renovation TV shows have glamorized our jobs. Now everyone wants to be hands-on."

"Worse, they think that because the shows make everything look so easy, they can do our jobs better than we can."

Josh and Eddie laughed together at a shared memory. They'd met when they'd been hired to work on a nearly destroyed old house back in New York. The homeowners had taken sledgehammers to most of the walls, not knowing if any were load-bearing before removing them. They'd also tried to move the plumbing stack, which had resulted in sewage being spewed all over the place. It was only after the house had practically collapsed that they'd sought professional help. Josh and Eddie had been part of the team that had restored the house. Eddie enjoyed working as a plumber, but he wasn't opposed to running a jobsite in Josh's absence.

"I still don't get it. There are plenty of doctor shows on TV, but you don't see people performing surgery on themselves."

"True," Eddie agreed with a chuckle. "I guess we're just lucky that way."

They stepped inside the house, leaving all mirth behind them as they focused on business. Josh talked with the different tradespeople who were on-site, inspected their work and made sure everyone had everything they needed. When he was done there, he checked on two more sites. On the first, the crew was updating a kitchen, family room and two baths.

The job was nearly finished and Josh was in and out of the site in under thirty minutes. The second job, a restoration he was doing for an insurance company, was more extensive. A fire had ripped through an old mansion, destroying all of the first floor and most of the second and third floors. It was a massive job and one Josh had been happy to land, thanks to his family's recommendation. Working on this old house was a joy and he'd even arranged his schedule so he could do a good deal of the carpentry himself.

When he was finished checking on sites, he stopped by his house, took a shower and put on a clean shirt and jeans. The rain had stopped and the sun was shining brightly. Most of the rain from earlier had dried, leaving little evidence of the storm that had ripped through town only hours earlier. There wasn't a cloud in the sky, so he didn't have to worry about a cloudburst drenching him. There was no way he was going to show up at Kirby's looking like a drowned dog a second time.

It was nearing lunchtime and his stomach grumbled. He imagined that Kirby and Lily would be hungry, too, and he didn't know what Kirby had planned for them to eat for lunch. After all, she had expected Lily to eat at school.

Josh pulled into a fast-food drive-through. He didn't know Lily well, but his siblings' and cousins' kids all loved chicken nuggets and fries. Especially when they were accompanied by a toy.

The aroma of the food filled the truck and he was raring to eat by the time he stepped inside the coffee shop. Most of the people who had been there earlier were now gone, leaving only the redheaded woman who was typing on her laptop and a guy sitting near the front window reading a book with a pastry and coffee cup in front of him.

Lily was sitting at the table they'd shared, playing with a doll. Kirby was wiping the counters. She looked up and smiled at him and he hoped that meant she was just as happy to see him as he was to see her.

"Hi. What do you have there?"

"I come bearing gifts," he said, closing the distance between them.

Lily had heard his voice, and she walked over to them, her doll clutched in her arms. "Hi, Josh. What's that?"

"I thought that you might be a little bit hungry, so I picked up lunch." He glanced at Kirby and for a moment he regretted being so impulsive. What if she didn't let her daughters eat fast food? "I hope it's okay."

"It's fine." She looked at Lily. "Let's go wash our hands."

While they did that, Josh put the food on the table Lily had been sitting at. The customer who'd been reading finished his coffee and then left. When Kirby returned, they sat down to eat. She opened Lily's barbecue sauce and ketchup packet.

"I love nuggets," Lily said, dipping the chicken into her sauce and then taking a big bite.

"So do my nephews," Josh said.

He hadn't known what to get Kirby, and debated the menu options. In the end, he'd decided to be wild and ordered her a burger and fries to match his.

Kirby dipped a couple of fries into the ketchup and put them into her mouth. After a few moments she smiled at him. "I usually eat healthy, but I must admit you have found my weakness."

"Will you think less of me if I admit to eating more than my share of fast food?"

"Heck, no. I imagine that with your job you spend a lot of time away from home and your stove."

"I have been pretty busy lately. But it's not work that keeps me from cooking. It's a total lack of skill."

"Accompanied by a total lack of interest?" she asked, raising a perfectly shaped eyebrow.

He laughed. "Yep. I don't want to spend the little free time I have in the kitchen. Lucky for me there are a few good restaurants in Rambling Rose, including two owned by my cousins."

They talked a bit more while they ate. He noticed that she didn't ask about the Fortunes. Was that because she'd heard about the animosity his father held for the wealthier Fortunes and thought he might share those feelings? He didn't. Josh didn't envy them their lifestyles or the fact that they'd gotten a head start in life that he hadn't received. Life was too short to be consumed by negativity. Besides, as he'd gotten to know his family, he discovered that they were really nice people and he enjoyed their company.

Or maybe her reluctance to talk about anything personal didn't have anything to do with him. Perhaps it was her way of keeping a barrier between them. After all, if she kept things casual, he would have to do the same or risk coming across as a jerk. So there was no way for him to get any of his questions answered. Like was there a Mr. Harris? Or any other man in her life?

When they finished eating, he stood and grabbed his trash. She covered his hand with hers. Her skin was smooth as silk, and he wanted to caress her fingers. That would be a bit presumptuous given the fact that they barely knew each other, so he resisted the urge. "I'll take care of that," she told him.

"Thanks. I'll check on the roof now that it's stopped raining."

"I appreciate it. Are you sure I can't pay you?"

"No. A delicious cup of cappuccino was my going rate this morning."

"All right," Kirby said. "But if you change your mind, let me know."

As he inspected the roof, he wondered if instead of settling for a cup of coffee, he should have asked for a date. But before he took that leap, he needed to find out more about her. If she wasn't involved with anyone, he was going to make his move. After assuring Kirby that all looked good on the roof, he said his goodbyes and went back to work.

When he got home that evening, he nuked a microwave dinner, opened a prepackaged salad and called his sister, Arabella. She was newly married and the one person he knew who could advise him on affairs of the heart. He loved his brothers, but although they were all married now, he didn't know if they had the information he needed. Besides, if they did, they'd give him a hard time, something he hoped to avoid.

"You got a minute?" he asked as soon as Arabella answered the phone.

"For my favorite brother? Of course."

They laughed together. He and his brothers had always referred to Arabella, their only sister, as their *favorite* sister, so she'd taken to referring to each of them as her favorite brother. But Josh had always insisted to Brian, Brady, Kane and Adam that she meant it when speaking about him.

"I didn't want anything in particular. Just to catch up."

"Okay."

He heard the skepticism in her voice, but she

didn't call him out. As she caught him up on her day, he listened and relaxed. It felt good knowing that his sister was so happy. She deserved every moment of joy she'd found. When she'd finished updating him, she turned the conversation back to him. "So what's up with you?"

"Oh, the usual. Working. Kane called me today and asked me to help the owner of the shop where he gets his coffee. Kirby Harris." He tried to sound nonchalant as he said Kirby's name and then explained about repairing her roof. "I've never been there before. The cappuccino she made for me was the best I've ever had."

"I'm not surprised. She's known for her coffee."

"Do you know much about her?"

"I know some. I've gone to her coffee shop quite a few times and we've talked on occasion. She's great. Kirby's Perks is a second home to a lot of people. She has a lot of regulars who wouldn't dream of getting their coffee anywhere else."

He'd seen that for himself.

Obviously he wasn't going to find out what he wanted to know by beating around the bush and hoping his sister finally hit upon the right subject. He took a deep breath and then blurted out his question. "Do you know if she's married or involved? She wasn't wearing a ring."

"Kirby's a widow. Her husband died a few years ago."

"Oh." He hadn't expected that. Kirby was so young to have lost a husband.

"But I have no clue whether or not she's currently dating anyone."

"Oh." That was disappointing.

"You're asking a lot of questions about Kirby. What gives?"

Josh wasn't ready to talk about that, even with Arabella. She might not tease him as their brothers would, but she was fully aware of his tendency to lead with his heart. "I was just curious."

That even sounded lame to him, but Arabella didn't push him.

He decided to change the subject. "Do you know if anyone else got a gift?"

"Not that I've heard."

Over the past few months, members of his family had been receiving anonymous gifts. The presents were odd to say the least. His brother Brady had received an old bust of a horse's head that had a secret compartment, where they'd found a key to a safe-deposit box in Austin. The box had held a poem and the initials *MAF*.

Around the same time, their cousin Bella had received a framed picture of a rose. The inscription had included the letters *MAF*.

Draper had received a calypso album. One of the songs had been about someone named Mary Ann.

Their cousin Beau had received a baby blanket with the initial *F* on it. Nobody knew what the gifts were supposed to mean, or if they meant anything. Taken alone, they were strange. Added together, they were a mystery the family had yet to be able to solve.

"I don't know if that's good or not. If nobody else gets one, then we might not get the entire picture or know who's behind all of this."

"There's still a chance. Maybe you might get one."

"I'm not so sure I want one. But if I do get a gift, I'll be sure to let everyone know."

Bella laughed. "Chicken."

"You'd better believe it," Josh said. "Have you heard from Mariana about the DNA test?"

"No. I'm sure she'll let us know when she gets the results."

Mariana was a middle-aged woman who'd lived in Rambling Rose for years and was beloved by the entire community. Her mother was deceased and she didn't know anything about her father. She'd also been the recipient of a baby blanket with the letter *F* on it. With the initials *MAF* and the calypso song with the name Mary Ann in the title, they'd all begun to wonder if the gifts were hinting that Mariana was a Fortune. They'd all thought—and Mariana had agreed—it was a good idea for her to take a DNA test so they could be sure.

"Maybe that's what all of the gifts are trying to tell us," Josh said. They'd discussed this before, but he couldn't help feeling there was more to it than this. Only time would tell.

They chatted for a few more minutes before saying good-night. After Josh ended the call, he sat for a while, contemplating his next move. If he wanted to know about Kirby, he was going to have to do what he should have done in the first place. He had to go to the source.

He might not know everything he wanted to know about her, but he'd learned one thing today. She might be friendly, but she also was guarded. And private. He knew he would have to take his time to get to know her. But he was a patient man. Which was good because he had a feeling he was going to need every ounce of patience he possessed.

"Time for bed," Kirby said as she stepped into the girls' bedroom.

"Five more minutes?" Violet said, looking up from the dollhouse, a tiny table in her hand. "I want to play some more."

Kirby sighed. Violet was not a morning person and getting her up for school was a huge hassle. She always whined and pulled the pillow over her head, begging for those *five more minutes* she wanted now. Kirby glanced over at Lily, who was snoring softly in her bed. Lily had conked out mere minutes after her head hit her pillow and before Kirby had finished reading their bedtime story.

"You said that five minutes ago."

Violet rolled her eyes. "I only need five more minutes."

Kirby stared at Violet, silently sending the message that it was bedtime. Her oldest daughter would argue from now until sunrise if given the opportunity. When Kirby didn't respond, Violet sighed dramatically, dropped the plastic table onto the floor, and rose. "Fine."

She flounced to her bed and knelt, whispering her prayers. When she finished, she climbed into the bed, shoved the pillow out of the way and placed her head on her mattress. "How many more days of school?"

"Not many."

"When it's summer vacation can I stay up as long as I want?"

"No. But I'll move bedtime back an hour or so. How's that?"

Violet's face twisted as she fought to hide a yawn. Kirby hid a smile, waiting until her daughter answered. "Okay."

Kirby kissed Violet's cheek and then left the room. No doubt Violet would be asleep within minutes.

Kirby returned to the living room and sat on the couch. Nighttime was when she missed her husband the most. Once the girls had been put to bed, she and Will used to sit close together and talk about their days or whatever else was on their minds. They'd never run out of things to talk about. Kirby had a loving family and a circle of friends, including her best-friend Ginny, that she spent time with, but she missed having that special someone in her life. The person who would be by her side through the good and bad. The person who would understand how she felt and know what she was thinking just by looking at the expression on her face.

Although the worst of her mourning was over and Kirby no longer felt the heaviness that had been her steady companion in the months after Will's death, she still felt his absence. Would there ever be a time when another man could fit in her life?

An image of Josh flashed in her mind, startling her. She'd just met him. Not only that, she didn't know a thing about him. Well, that wasn't entirely true. In the short time they'd spent together she'd learned that he was a considerate man. A hardworking man. That he didn't wait to be asked before helping. He'd jumped right in so that she could keep her coffee shop open when she'd gone to get Lily. She also knew that he kept his word. He'd said that he would come back to check on her roof and he had, even bringing lunch with him.

Josh had won Lily over immediately. Long after he'd left that afternoon, she'd talked about how nice he was. How much he'd liked her stories. Of course, the chicken nuggets had helped gain her daughter's favor.

Not that any of it mattered. He could be married or involved, for all Kirby knew. Besides, her heart might have healed from the terrible loss of Will, but she wasn't ready to give it over to anyone right now. The risk of being devastated again was far too great. She had her daughters and her business.

That would have to be enough.

Chapter Three

"I'll take a cappuccino."

Kirby looked up at Josh and smiled. He looked so good in a T-shirt that stretched across his broad shoulders and chest before tapering down to his smooth stomach. No doubt about it, he was the best-looking man she'd seen in years and the nicest she'd encountered in just as long. "Okay. It's on the house."

"Nonsense." He pulled out his wallet and removed his debit card. Before she could stop him, he placed it in the reader.

"I'm surprised to see you here today."

"Don't be. After that cappuccino you made for me yesterday, I don't think I'll ever be able to drink a bland cup of coffee again. You've spoiled me and now I won't settle for anything other than the best."

His words sent a thrill down her spine. She knew he'd been talking about cappuccino, and yet somehow, she sensed that he was talking about more than that. He'd been talking about her. But that was ridiculous. It had to be her overactive imagination reading way too much into his simple words. "I'm glad you enjoyed it. Do you want anything to go with your drink?"

He flashed her a wicked grin and she knew she hadn't been imagining things. He was flirting with her. "How about one of those crullers?"

"No problem." She completed his order and reluctantly accepted his payment. He carried his drink and pastry to a table near the window where he could look out at the passing cars.

Rambling Rose had changed quite a bit over the past few years. Kirby had grown up here, and apart from the four years she'd spent at Howard University she hadn't lived anywhere else. Although many of the changes were considered improvements, she was frequently nostalgic for the town of her youth. There was something to be said for the quaint, old-fashioned if slightly run-down Rambling Rose. Now there was a fancy hotel and a gated community filled with enormous mansions. And millionaires. The Fortunes had definitely made their mark on the town.

But time marched on. Either you went with the tide, or you were swept away. So she looked for the good in the modern changes and ignored the rest.

A steady stream of customers kept her and Hillary, her sixtyish barista, busy for a while, leaving little time for reminiscing about the past. Or sneaking peeks at Josh.

When there was a lull, she cleaned tables and made her way to Josh. He'd finished his drink and cruller, but he didn't seem in any big hurry to leave. Given that it was a beautiful day, it couldn't be because there was no work for him to do. This was perfect construction weather.

"While I'm here," he said when she was standing beside his table, "I want to take another look at your roof."

"Again?"

"Yes. I know I checked yesterday afternoon, but it should be completely dry today. I just want to look around. That is, if it's okay."

"You're the professional."

"So I am," he said with a wink. "I'll be right back."

She tried not to read anything into that wink, but it took some effort. Shaking her head, she wiped his table and then returned to the counter.

Hillary gave her a knowing look. "That's one good-looking man."

"Josh? I suppose he's okay. That is if you go for that type."

"If you mean the sexy-without-trying, built-like-Adonis, good-with-his-hands type? Sign me up." Hillary shook her head. "If I was only a few years younger, I'd be fighting you for him."

"Me? There's nothing going on between Josh and me."

Hillary put a gentle hand on Kirby's shoulder. "It's okay to move on. Will loved you deeply and wanted only the best for you. He would want you to find happiness with another man who could be a good stepfather for those two little angels of yours."

"I know he would. He told me as much before he…died. But that doesn't mean I have to throw myself at the first man who looks my way."

"If you think he's the first man to look your way, then you haven't been paying attention."

Sure, men had approached her from time to time, but they hadn't stuck around. All she needed to do was mention that she had two daughters and the men magically disappeared, taking their unwanted attention with them. And she had bid them a hasty goodbye. As a single mother she needed to be careful whom she got involved with, screening out the good men from those looking for a good time. She wouldn't bring a man into her life who didn't love her little girls as if they were his own. Will had adored them. If another man wasn't willing or able to do the same, he could keep on stepping.

Excusing herself, Kirby grabbed her purse and went to the ladies' room, where she combed her hair then replaced the headband holding it out of her face. Telling herself she wasn't suddenly interested in her appearance because Josh was around, but rather because she wanted to be presentable, she dug out her lipstick and brushed it across her lips. Most days she didn't bother with makeup, but where was the harm in a little lipstick? She straightened her apron and then returned to the front of the shop. She could hear Josh walking around on her roof, and with each footstep she heard, she began to wonder if he'd discovered another problem.

A few minutes later the sound stopped, and he stepped inside.

"What's the diagnosis?"

"It's in good shape and should survive any other rainstorms with no problem."

"That's a relief. But I have another question."

"Shoot."

"Is there still water in the ceiling?" She looked up. Dingy rings appeared where the water had poured through yesterday.

"I can check it for you. And even if a little remains I should be able to take care of that quite easily."

"I know you're a carpenter but you wouldn't by

any chance like to paint, too, would you? If not, perhaps you can recommend someone to paint over the water stains. I don't want my place to start looking shabby."

"Not to worry. I can take care of that and any other jobs that need doing." He checked his watch. "I actually have a job to get to now, but if you're free this evening, I can come back and take a look at your ceiling and let you know what you're dealing with."

"I don't have plans."

"Great. How does six sound? Too late?"

"You're doing me the favor, so I'll work with your schedule. Whatever works for you works for me."

"It's not a favor if I inconvenience you."

"Six is fine."

"I'll see you then."

After Josh left, Kirby tried hard to focus on her shop, but it was harder than she would have expected. Every time there was a lull, images of Josh filled her mind. When traffic inside slowed to a trickle, Hillary grabbed her purse. She generally only worked until about twelve thirty, before she headed out to spend the rest of the day doing whatever struck her fancy. Hillary had never married or had children, but she had the most fulfilling life of anyone Kirby had ever met. In the time that Kirby had known her, Hillary had gone skydiving and studied to be a hot-air balloon pilot. Now she was learning how to scuba dive.

Kirby didn't know if she would ever be as adventurous as Hillary, but she hoped she would enjoy life as much when she was that age.

"You seem happy," Martin said as she approached his table.

"I'm always happy," Kirby replied, sitting across from him.

"Oh, but there's a bit of a glow to your face. Could it be that young man who fixed the roof yesterday and who just happened to stop by today?"

"Josh? He's just a friend. Not even that really. We just met."

"Is that so? That blush on your cheeks tells a different story."

Kirby pressed her hands to her hot face.

Martin chuckled and picked up his cup. "I guess I have my answer."

Kirby rose and patted Martin on his shoulder. "I think you're seeing more than what's there."

"Maybe so. But I'm going to be keeping an eye on that fellow just to be sure."

"There's no need to do that."

"No reason not to, either," he replied and then picked up his newspaper, putting an end to the conversation. Before long it was time for Kirby to close the shop for the day and pick up the girls from school. She pulled into the parking lot and then joined the rest of the parents clustered together on the edge of the parking lot. She made small talk with several of the other mothers until the children emerged from the school.

Violet's class was released first and she ran over to Kirby with her arms outstretched. Kirby hugged her and kissed her cheek. "How was school?"

"It was the b-e-s-t day ever. I won the s-p-e-l-l-i-n-g bee."

"Good for you."

"We even had words from the next chapter and I got them all right so I know I'm going to get an A on the next spelling test. Ms. Robinson even used some third-grade words. I won a pretty pencil and an eraser that looks like a pencil. It's in my pencil pouch now, but I'll show it to you when we get home."

"That's wonderful. All of your hard work paid off."

"Yep. Anthony was jealous because he kept telling me he was the best speller. But I won."

Anthony Woods and Violet had been locked in a serious battle for the best grades ever since kindergarten. Each of them was seriously competitive and didn't like coming in second place. So far, they'd each won about half of the time. Fortunately their academic quest hadn't interfered with their friendship.

While they were talking, Lily's teacher escorted her students to the parking lot. The other children dashed to their parents, but Lily walked slowly behind them, her head down. Clearly something was troubling her. Kirby glanced at Mrs. Bennett, who shrugged and shook her head. No help there.

Kirby hugged and kissed Lily, then lifted her daughter's chin so she could look into her eyes. "How was school?"

"Okay."

"Really?"

Lily nodded against Kirby's hand.

"If something happened, would you tell me?"

Lily shrugged.

Kirby was frustrated with that response, but she couldn't badger her child. Clearly Lily wasn't willing to share her feelings yet and Kirby was just going to have to wait until she was. But then, maybe nothing was wrong and Kirby was reading too much into Lily's behavior. Kirby had her moments of ennui; so could Lily. It was unreasonable to expect her child to be happy all the time. And she certainly didn't want to teach Lily to fake joy or any other emotion in order to please Kirby. So she let the subject drop. Taking Lily's hand, she led her to the car.

She and the girls had developed an afterschool routine. The minute they stepped inside the house, the girls changed into play clothes, washed their hands and then came into the kitchen for their snack. When they finished, they did their homework, then went out to play.

Later that afternoon, as they sat down to dinner of lasagna and salad, one of their favorite meals, they chatted about their respective days.

Violet was still exhilarated over her victory in the spelling bee and told the story to Lily, who was dutifully impressed. Lily laughed as Violet mimicked the frown on Anthony's face when he misspelled *beautiful.*

"I hope I'm a good speller like you when I'm in second grade," Lily said wistfully.

"Don't worry. I'll help you study if you need me to. That way you can win a pretty pencil. You can use mine if you want. You just have to ask first."

"Thanks, Violet," Lily said sincerely.

Suddenly Kirby's eyes filled with tears and she had to blink them back before they fell. Her daughters were such good girls. They might squabble at times as all siblings did, but when push came to shove, they were there for each other. Will would be so pleased to see what wonderful children he'd helped create. Her heart ached when she thought about how much of their lives he had missed. How much more he would miss.

But there was no sense in brooding over what she couldn't change. And really, she didn't know why she was behaving this way. She'd long ago accepted Will's death and had focused on making a life for herself and her girls. So why was today any different? Why were thoughts of Will suddenly consuming her?

Perhaps it's because of Josh.

The thought was so sudden that she nearly dropped her fork onto her empty plate. And it was entirely ridiculous. What did Josh Fortune have to do with her life? They barely knew each other. Sure, she found him attractive, but that didn't mean she was about to become romantically involved with him.

Still, Josh Fortune was the first man she'd noticed as a *man* since she'd lost Will. And she wasn't sure how she felt about that. She didn't want him intruding in her life, commandeering her thoughts, barging into her quiet and safe world. She sighed. If she was being honest, he hadn't done anything of the sort. She was the one who'd asked him to stop by the store this evening. And if she couldn't stop thinking about him, that was on her.

Speaking of Josh Fortune, she had an appointment to get to.

"Girls, we need to go to the coffee shop."

"Why?" Violet asked. "Isn't it closed?"

"I have someone coming to check on some work. It won't take long. Then we can go to the park to play."

The girls hurried to get ready. They enjoyed coming to the coffee shop with her and when they were younger, they'd often accompanied her on days when she didn't have a babysitter. In the beginning, she'd felt guilty about dragging them with her, but they'd genuinely seemed to have fun. Even so, she closed the coffee shop early and didn't open at all on Sunday so the girls could have some semblance of a normal childhood.

She drove the short distance to the coffee shop and was just unlocking the front door when Josh drove into the lot and parked his pickup truck beside her car.

Lily smiled and waved when she saw him. "Hi, Josh."

"Hi, Lily," he called as he approached them. He smiled and Kirby's foolish heart did a little dance. Not going to happen, she reminded herself. Not with Josh or anyone else.

"Who's that?" Violet asked. She frowned and looked suspiciously from Kirby to Josh. Clearly she wasn't going to be won over as easily as Lily had been.

"That's Josh," Lily said before Kirby could reply. "He's me and Mommy's friend. I bet he would be your friend, too, if you want."

Violet's frown grew as she pushed the door open and stepped inside, immediately running to get a toy from the office.

"Are you who we're waiting on?" Lily asked.

"Yes, I am. I hope that's okay with you," Josh said sincerely.

"Yep. I like seeing you." Lily took his hand and swung it back and forth, looking at Josh with what could only be described as adoration.

"Let's play checkers," Violet said, returning to the room carrying the box in her arms.

"Wait a minute, Violet," Kirby said, placing a hand on her daughter's shoulder as she passed by. "I want you to meet Mr. Fortune. He's here to help me with the shop."

Violet stopped and then looked at Josh. "Hi."

Kirby was surprised at the coolness she heard in her daughter's voice.

"It's very nice to meet you, Violet," Josh said politely, as if her daughter hadn't just given him the cold shoulder.

Violet merely turned to her sister. "Come on, Lily. Let's go play."

"Okay." Lily grinned at Josh again before following her sister to a table.

"Let me apologize for my daughter's behavior."

"Don't. Some kids are friendlier than others. My siblings and I all have different personalities. She's entitled to feel whatever she wants about me."

"Maybe. But she doesn't have to be rude about it."

"She's a kid with limited life experiences and

therefore has limited ways of expressing herself. I'm good with that."

"Wow. You're pretty savvy about little kids for a bachelor."

He grinned. "Well, my siblings and cousins have lots of kids so I'm around them a lot. And to be honest, what little knowledge I have, I picked up from hanging around my brother Brady. He became the guardian for twin boys about Lily's age. He's a great dad."

Josh made good points. But then, he didn't know that Violet was generally a friendly child who liked all of Kirby's friends. But then, all of Kirby's friends were women or the spouses of her friends. Josh didn't fit into either category. For whatever reason, she'd taken an instant dislike to him.

Kirby glanced at the girls who had started their game. Lily put a finger on a piece and then looked at Violet, who shook her head. Immediately Lily lifted her finger and placed it on another checker. When Violet nodded, Lily slid the piece to another square.

"Good move," Violet said approvingly.

Assured that her daughters were getting along, Kirby turned to Josh. "Come on, I'll show you what needs to be done and you can let me know if it's in your wheelhouse."

"In my *wheelhouse*?" He laughed, a low, sexy sound that raised goose bumps on her arms.

"Is that not the right word?"

"I know what you meant. And let me assure you, whatever you need to have done, I'm quite capable of handling. I'm your man."

Josh watched as Kirby's eyes widened before she looked away. Did he just say that? Sure, he'd meant to say that he could do whatever job needed doing, but somehow it hadn't come out that way. Instead it had come across as flirtatious. He wondered if he should say something to clean up the mess he'd made but decided not to try. As clumsy as his words had been, he'd probably only make the situation worse. The last thing he wanted to do was make Kirby feel uncomfortable around him.

But he didn't want the awkward moment to drag on, either. "So…you mentioned checking to be sure there was no more water in the ceiling and also painting it? I can check for water today, too."

She blew out what he perceived as a relieved breath and then pointed up at the water rings. "I don't want a constant reminder of that disastrous day."

"I wouldn't say the entire day was disastrous," Josh said with a grin. "You did make my acquaintance."

She grinned as he'd hoped she would. "Well, there is that. I stand corrected. I should say I don't want to remember seeing water pouring through my ceiling and dripping onto everything below. Including customers."

He looked at the ceiling. Although the rings weren't all that bad, the ceiling could use a fresh coat of paint. In fact, although the coffee shop was charming, the entire place could use a refresh. "What color were you thinking of?"

"I like the cream color of the walls." She looked around and he followed her gaze to the light brown tables and the striped upholstery on the chairs and booths. There were several watercolors hanging on the walls that he hadn't noticed before. Perhaps Kirby had removed them to keep them from being damaged. "I don't want to make a drastic change that would require me to redo the rest of the decor."

Josh nodded. "Do you remember the name of the paint?"

"No. Will picked it out."

"Will?"

"My late husband. He painted it as a surprise for me." She smiled softly and her eyes took on a faraway look. He imagined she was reliving fond memories of him.

"He sounds like he was a good guy."

"The best."

Well, there was no competing with that. But then, this wasn't a competition. After all, he was only getting to know Kirby, not diving into the deep end as he'd done in the past, hoping the woman would jump in beside him. He was going to be smart—leading with his head and not his heart. He was going to be her friend first and see what—if anything—developed.

"If you want, I can pick up some paint samples and bring them by tomorrow. It shouldn't be too hard to match the color your husband used. The question is, when would be the best time for me to paint?"

"You're really going to paint the ceiling for me?"

"Not just the ceiling. I'm going to paint the walls, too. The shop isn't all that big. I can knock it out in a couple of days."

She hesitated, clearly reluctant. "I don't know..." She looked around and by her expression he knew she was taking in the stains and wear and tear on the walls. But it had to be her decision. And given the fact that her late husband had done the painting, he knew it was going to be an emotional one.

"Why don't I go check to make sure there's not still water in the ceiling while you think about it."

She nodded and he left her alone. It only took a few minutes for him to check everything. Luckily, no water remained.

"How's the ceiling?" she asked when he returned.

"Everything's fine."

"Thank goodness."

"What about the walls?"

"Hmm. I guess it will be all right," she said slowly.

"And they do need a fresh coat of paint. I can close for a couple days. And if we work together, it won't take that long."

"You want to help?"

"Yes."

"Do you know how to paint?"

"About as well as you work a cappuccino machine."

He laughed. "In my defense, the machine had a lot of buttons and gizmos."

"And painting only requires paint and a roller."

"And drop cloths, and tape, and cut-in brushes, and—"

She waved her hand dismissively and gave him a cheeky grin. "I'll leave the hard parts to you. I'll just roll the paint on the walls."

There was no way he was going to say no to an opportunity to spend more time with her, even if it meant the job might take longer than usual—or especially because it might take longer. "That sounds like a plan."

"How much do you charge?"

He should have expected the question. Although he had only met her, it was easy to tell that Kirby was an independent woman. Perhaps because as a widow she'd been forced to fend for herself in a lot of situations. Even though the inquiry hurt his feelings a bit, he understood. He supported himself in the construction business. It only made sense that she'd figure he would charge her for his labor. To her, this was a business deal. To him, it was the beginning of a friendship.

"A cappuccino a day for a month."

She laughed. "Be serious, Josh."

His name sounded good on her lips and he savored the moment before answering. "I am being serious. I told you that your coffee is the best I've ever had. I'm definitely getting the better of the deal here."

"Josh." She sounded slightly aggravated.

"Let's call it the friends and family discount. We are becoming friends, aren't we?"

She flashed a mischievous grin. "I suppose you're growing on me."

He laughed. "I'll take that. But if it makes you feel better, you can throw in a cruller or doughnut every day."

"Deal." She extended her hand, and he took it. Her skin was so soft and warm. He could definitely get used to her touch. The temptation to cover her hand with his other one was great, and it took monumental effort to suppress it. He didn't want to be too forward, so he released her hand.

"I'd hate to inconvenience my regulars, but I think a weekday will work best. That way my girls will be in school and not underfoot. I just need a couple of days to let everyone know that I'll be closed. Will next Monday work for you?"

"Yes." As they stood there staring at each other, Josh tried to think of something to say to prolong the moment, but nothing came to mind. They'd accomplished everything they'd set out to do, so there was no reason for them to hang around any longer. But she didn't make an effort to move, either. Perhaps she was as reluctant to say good-night as he was.

"I win!"

At Lily's gleeful cry, Kirby blinked and stepped back. It was as if her daughter's voice had broken a spell, reminding Kirby that they weren't alone. Her brow wrinkled as she tried to pick up the broken threads of their conversation. "That sounds good. I guess I'll see you tomorrow. I need to get going. I promised the girls we'd stop by the park for a few minutes."

"Sure."

She walked over to the table where her daughters had been playing checkers. Her hips swayed with each step, and he admired her sexy bottom before looking away. His eyes met Violet's. She gave him a hard stare before turning her attention back to her younger sister, who was still exultant about her victory.

"I beat Violet in checkers."

"You did? That's wonderful," Kirby said, hugging

her younger daughter. “It’s time for us to leave. Put the game away.”

“Are we still going to the park?” Lily asked.

“For a bit.”

“It’s just us three, right?” Violet asked, glaring at him briefly before looking back at Kirby. “*He’s* not coming, is he?”

“His name is Josh, and no, he’s not coming.”

“Good. I like it when it’s just us three.”

“I like Josh,” Lily said as she dropped the last checker into the box. “He’s my friend.”

Violet didn’t reply, but he could tell by her silence that she didn’t consider him a friend. His experience with little girls might be limited to his nieces and his cousins’ kids, who actually adored him, but it was clear that she viewed him as an interloper. Someone intruding on her family.

Once the game was put away, Kirby set the alarm and they all stepped outside. The sun was not high in the sky, but there was still daylight left. He walked Kirby and her girls to their car, then leaned against his truck. He waited until they’d pulled away before he climbed in his truck and drove off. A part of him wished that he was accompanying them to the park, but he ignored it. This was family time, and he wasn’t a member of their family. Still, he couldn’t deny the sudden loneliness that gripped him as he returned to his empty house.

Growing up as one of six kids who were close in age, there had always been someone around to hang out with. Josh had always been a bit more independent, often doing things on his own, but he had always known one of his brothers or his sister was around if he wanted company.

Now, though, his siblings were all happily married and building lives of their own. He was glad that they'd each found love and that their lives were full. And he knew that they would welcome him for dinner or to watch the games at any time. But that wasn't what he wanted. For the first time in his life, being on his own was bothering him. And he knew why.

He wanted a family of his own.

Chapter Four

Kirby dusted her hands on her jeans as excitement swept through her. She'd dropped the girls at school on Monday morning and then come directly to the coffee shop. As he'd promised, Josh had come by a couple of days ago and brought several paint samples in a range of colors for her to consider. At first she had intended to match the cream paint that Will had used all those years ago, but her eye kept gravitating to the darker sample. Finally she'd decided to go with a new color. It would still work with the decor.

She'd given Josh a spare key and he'd come by last night and moved the furniture out of the main room and into the kitchen and storage room. What wouldn't fit, he'd pushed to one side of the dining room and out of the way.

The bell over the front door jingled and she looked up. Since she'd notified her regular customers and put up a sign that she would be closing for two days, that could only mean one thing. Josh was here.

She ran a hand over her hair, making sure that not one strand had escaped her ponytail. Ordinarily she wore her hair down around her shoulders held back by a headband, but she didn't want to risk getting paint in it. She'd considered covering it with a bandanna, but she'd quickly shot down the notion. Even though there was absolutely nothing remotely romantic going on between her and Josh, she still wanted to look her best around him. Which was why she'd brushed her eyelashes with mascara and dabbed a little bit of gloss on her lips this morning.

"Hey," she said as he stepped inside.

"Hey," he replied. He put a five-gallon paint bucket against the door to hold it open.

"What else do you have?" she asked as she crossed the room. "Do you need help with anything?"

"Sure. You can bring in the paint trays and rollers. I'll get the ladder and the drop cloths."

She followed him to his truck and grabbed the items he mentioned. It took two trips for them to get everything inside.

"I have my phone, if you want to listen to some

music," she said as they began to organize everything.

"Sure. What type of music do you like?"

"Good music."

He laughed. "I wouldn't expect anything else. But that tells me exactly nothing."

"I like Beyoncé, the Weeknd, Bruno Mars, Rihanna, Jazmine Sullivan. You know, good music."

"Ah." He nodded.

"Don't tell me you've never heard of them."

"Of course I've heard of them. I live in Texas now where country music is king, and I do like country singer Jett Carr, but I'm from Buffalo, New York." He grabbed a paintbrush, held it like a microphone and began to croon the latest Bruno Mars ballad.

He had a surprisingly good voice and as he sang the romantic words, butterflies began to dance in her stomach. After singing the chorus, he dipped his head in a playful bow. She applauded. It was fun to laugh and joke with Josh, even while painting.

"So are we listening to my playlist?" she asked him.

"Absolutely."

She switched on the music, playing it loud enough for them to enjoy, but not so loud that it would prevent them from talking to each other.

Josh showed her how to tape the wood trim around the windows. Once she knew what to do, he knelt down and began to tape the baseboards.

"I think I got it now," she said, taking the tape from him. It was a little harder than it looked to keep it straight and not go onto the wall. But working carefully, she was able to do it.

"I'm sure you do. And if it's not exactly perfect, don't worry about it. Just make sure to cover all of the trim. I can always paint any spots on the wall after we remove the tape."

They worked for a few minutes in silence before her curiosity got the better of her. "How old are you, Josh?"

"I'm twenty-eight."

Wow. He was so young. He didn't ask how old she was, so she volunteered the information. "I'm thirty-four."

"We're about the same age."

Not really. He was six years younger than she was. That might not be a big difference in ten years, but it was an enormous difference now.

"How long have you lived in Rambling Rose?" she asked.

"I moved here a couple of months ago. I guess you could say I followed my brothers and sister here."

"And do you like it?"

"So far so good."

"I imagine it must be a bit different from Buffalo. You must be experiencing culture shock."

He laughed. "I wouldn't go that far. But it is a bit

quieter here. Not as much nightlife. No sports bars to hang out in after work, and no clubs to go to on the weekends. I'm still getting used to that."

She realized that he was a fun-loving, free-as-a-bird bachelor and she was a single mother with responsibilities. He could spend his nights out on the town with friends, while apart from the occasional girls' night out, she spent her nights at home with her children.

Not that she would have it any other way. She loved spending time with her girls. And if she suffered occasional bouts of loneliness, well, that was to be expected.

Kirby finished taping the trim and looked around. Josh was staring at her and she realized he must have asked her a question that she'd failed to answer. She smiled. There was no sense in pretending that she'd heard what he'd said. "I'm sorry. I was miles away and didn't hear a word you said."

He shrugged and she couldn't keep her eyes from straying to his massive shoulders. He was dressed in a gray T-shirt that had green and orange paint spatters on it, and loose-fit jeans that fit him perfectly. There was no denying it. Josh was a hunk. "No worries. It wasn't anything earth-shattering."

"That's good to know. But I'm paying attention now if you don't mind repeating yourself."

He smiled and she barely stopped herself from

shivering. What was wrong with her? She hadn't looked at another man from the minute she and Will had gone on their first date. Yet here she was, standing in her place of business, gawking at Josh and salivating as if he were a box of her favorite chocolates.

"I asked if you wanted to listen to my playlist since yours ended."

"Oh. Sure. I'm curious about the type of music you like."

"I like good music." He grinned as he said it.

"I suppose I had that coming."

"Sorry. I couldn't resist." Then he explained, "I have eclectic tastes."

"What does that mean?"

"It means I listen to all kinds of music. Rock, pop, hip-hop, R & B. The occasional country song—I mean, Jett Carr is my brother-in-law so it's kind of expected. Even some classic bands."

"Classic like how? Please don't tell me I've just agreed to listen to heavy metal or big hair bands or whatever they're called."

"Do I look like that type?"

She shrugged. "I have no idea. I'm not sure what people who listen to that type of music look like."

He grabbed his phone and swiped at the screen. A moment later, the first strains of a song filled the air. She listened carefully. After a few notes she smiled.

"I take it you recognize this song."

"Of course. I don't think there's a person alive who doesn't know 'Hotel California.' My parents are big Eagles fans."

He paused the music and then tapped the screen. "How about this?"

It only took a few beats for her to recognize the song. She looked at him in surprise. "What do you know about Lizzo?"

He laughed. "Surprised?"

"Uh. Yeah."

"Why?"

She shrugged. "Okay. I get your point. You have good taste in music. It's actually similar to mine."

"Some things are universal. They aren't separated by age or race or religion. Music is one of them. Love is another."

She nodded her agreement. "You're right. So turn on your music and let's get busy painting."

He pushed a button on his phone and music filled the air. "Let me check your work."

"Don't trust me, huh?"

"Oh, I trust you, but you're a newbie. The last thing we want is for paint to get on your trim."

He inspected her work and smiled. "Not bad."

"Not bad?" She placed her hands on her hips. "Admit it. I did a great job."

"If I say that, you might get a big head. And we wouldn't want that."

She nudged him with her shoulder and he laughed. "Okay, you did a great job."

"That's right." She danced around chanting, "I did a great job. I did a great job."

Josh poured the paint into two trays and carried one to the windowless wall. "This is for you. I'll do the walls by the windows. Less chance of getting paint on the glass."

She nodded and then dipped the roller into the paint. After removing the excess, she held the roller in her hand and stared at the wall. *Will painted this.*

"I imagine this must be difficult for you."

She turned at the sound of Josh's voice. She'd been so lost in her thoughts that she hadn't heard him approach.

"How did you know?"

"You told me that your husband painted the shop. It must feel like you're removing a trace of him by painting over it."

That was it exactly. "Do you think that's foolish?"

"Not at all. You loved him. If you don't want to repaint it, I can match the color and paint over the stains and call it a day."

"No. I need to repaint. Will would understand that. In fact, he'd probably laugh at me for getting all emotional about it." She could hear him now. *Go for it, baby. Make your place pretty.*

She could do this. Inhaling deeply, she stepped

up to the wall and then rolled on the paint. It was as if she was taking a step out of the past and into the present.

"Paint a *W*."

"What? I don't know what that means."

Josh stepped up to her and held out his hand. She gave him the roller, which he dipped into the tray, expertly coating it with paint and rolling off the excess. "May I?"

She nodded.

He handed her the roller and then covered her hand with his. Electricity shot from where their skin met and, immediately, each of her nerve endings went on high alert. His hands were callused, yet his touch was gentle. Stepping behind her, so close that the heat from his body reached out and caressed her, he guided her hand over the wall.

"Relax," he said softly.

She realized she was stiff as a board and blew out a breath. His nearness was doing all kinds of things to her body and his touch had her imagination running wild, filling her with sensual fantasies. She struggled to clear her mind so she could focus on his instructions. She loosened her arm and let him take the lead. In a few long strokes he had painted four long lines in the shape of the letter *W*.

"Now do you understand?"

She nodded, not trusting her voice.

"Once you have the *W* painted, you can fill in the space."

"I think I can handle it from here."

"Sure." As if realizing how close they were standing, he took a giant step back, then returned to his side of the room and picked up his paintbrush.

It took a moment before Kirby trusted herself to paint again. Her heart was pounding so hard she thought it might burst from her chest. She didn't know what it was, but there was something about Josh that sent her blood surging through her veins and made her want things she couldn't have. She frowned. She was too old to lie to herself. She was attracted to Josh and not simply because he had a gorgeous body and handsome face. She liked the way he treated her. She liked the way he understood the mixed emotions she was feeling now and didn't judge her for them.

She also liked the way he treated her daughters. Lily had adored him on sight. Who didn't want to be adored? He hadn't minded the way she had told him story upon story upon story. In fact, he seemed to enjoy her company. But it was easy to like someone who clearly liked you. But he hadn't been fazed by the fact that for a reason known only to herself, Violet had taken an instant dislike to him. He'd returned Violet's rudeness with kindness, letting her establish the boundaries of their relationship. Kirby appreciated his attitude more than she could say. She appreciated *him.*

Which worried her because her attraction to Josh was growing with each passing minute.

No!

She chided her rebellious body. Despite the attraction, she told herself she couldn't be interested in becoming involved with a man. And even if she were, Josh Fortune was all wrong for her. He was too young. Too carefree. There was no way he was ready for anything serious. Especially with a single mom.

So why did her heart sink with disappointment at the thought?

Josh returned to his side of the room, adjusted the drop cloth, which was already perfectly situated, and then picked up his brush and began cutting in around the windows. What in the world had possessed him to wrap his arms around Kirby that way? What had he been thinking? He hadn't been thinking. He'd been feeling.

From the moment he'd laid eyes on her this morning, he'd wanted to hold her close to him and feel her soft body against his. He'd longed to kiss her full lips and run his hands through her gorgeous, thick hair, all the while inhaling her sweet scent. But doing any of that was out of the question. He needed to stick to the plan and keep things light. Friendly. Get to know

Kirby. But when the opportunity to get closer to her presented itself, he'd been unable to resist.

His heart raced as he recalled how wonderful it had felt to be close to her. She'd smelled so good and with each breath he'd taken, his desire for her had grown until it was nearly out of control. He'd tried to disguise it, but he wasn't entirely sure he'd managed. Some things couldn't be hidden.

He inhaled and slowly blew out the breath. This was ridiculous. He'd never had this much difficulty being friends with a woman. True, he'd had the habit of falling in love fast, but that was all in the past. He'd moved to Rambling Rose for a fresh start. But starting over included more than a new town in a new state. It meant getting rid of bad habits and developing better ones. He'd suffered the last broken heart that he intended to have. He was going to be wiser. And that meant protecting his heart. No more thinking he was in love with a woman he barely knew and pursuing her with all he had in him. That foolishness was in the past. And he intended to keep it there. He was not only living in a new town. He was a new Josh.

They worked without talking for a while, the music of Michael Jackson and the Eagles melting into songs by Ed Sheeran, Drake and Whitney Houston.

"Oh, I love Whitney," Kirby said. "Turn that up, please."

"Sure." Josh strode across the room and increased the volume. When he turned around he noticed Kirby swiveling her hips and shaking her shoulders to "I Wanna Dance with Somebody."

She turned around and looked at him. "Don't tell me you've never seen anybody dance."

"Not on a jobsite," he admitted. And definitely no one who moved as well as she did.

She put down her roller and held out her hand. "Don't make me dance alone."

Setting down his brush, he closed the distance between them and did his best to keep up with her. Dancing wasn't his strong suit, but he liked to believe that he had rhythm and could stay on the beat. When she didn't break into gales of laughter as he danced, his confidence grew.

"Look at you," she said, shimmying as she came closer to him. She was so near that he wouldn't have to move more than an inch in her direction to touch her. Unable to resist, he took one of her hands into his and put his other hand on her waist. He could have stayed like this forever and been the happiest man alive, but sadly the song ended.

"Thank you for the dance," Josh said as she stepped away.

"The pleasure was mine. I haven't danced in the longest time."

"Well, it might be an oldie, but it's definitely a good song to dance to."

"Let me stop you right there," she said, holding up one slender finger. There was a smear of paint on her perfectly shaped nail. "What we not gon' do is disrespect Whitney Houston in this establishment."

"What?" He shook his head. What had he said?

"Whitney Houston's music is not now, nor will it ever be, classified as oldies."

"I meant that the song is a classic."

She shook her head and her lips compressed into a frown. Another swing and a miss. One more whiff and he'd be out.

"I got nothing," he finally said.

"Whitney was a legend. And her music is timeless," Kirby said slowly as if speaking to a child.

"Of course." He didn't want to risk striking out, so he changed the subject and circled back to something she'd said earlier. "Why haven't you danced in a long time? You're good at it and you obviously enjoy it."

The sparkle left her eyes and her shoulders slumped. He should have told her not to answer, but he really wanted to know her. Besides, sometimes it helped to talk about a painful subject with someone who cared.

"My husband and I used to dance all the time. Before the kids were born, we went out to clubs in Austin and met up with friends on weekends. After

Violet was born, we stopped going out and started dancing at home. We'd go all out. We'd cook a great dinner, turn down the lights and turn up the music. It might have just been the two of us, but it was a real party. I haven't danced since he died."

"Until today."

She nodded. "Until today. With you."

He tried not to read too much into that statement, but a small seed of hope planted itself in his heart. Maybe she was attracted to him as much as he was to her. "Well, you're a great dancer. You should make time to dance again. In fact, you should make time for all things that you enjoy. Fun is good."

"You're right. Fun is good. But I have responsibilities. I can't let myself forget that." She straightened her shoulders, picked up her roller and started painting again.

He didn't know what he'd said wrong, so he replayed the conversation in his mind. Nothing stood out, but he knew he'd killed the mood. After a moment, he picked up his brush and began painting, too. Hopefully he'd find the right thing to say to get that fun feeling back.

Chapter Five

"Break time," Kirby said, setting her roller in the tray. They'd been working steadily for two hours. She hadn't realized until this moment just how large her coffee shop was. Although they'd been painting at a fairly good clip, there was still a lot of painting left to do. Rubbing her aching shoulders, she glanced over at Josh.

"If you say so, boss."

She laughed. He'd been calling her *boss* all morning and it still tickled her funny bone, as her dad liked to say. "I do."

"If you want, I can go out and grab us a couple of sandwiches."

"How about we both go? That way we can eat outside and enjoy the fresh air."

"I can get with that. I'll take care of things in here while you wash your hands."

She nodded. Although she'd thought she'd been careful, she'd still managed to get paint on her hands and arms as well as her clothes. Stepping into the bathroom and looking in the mirror, she added her face to the list of paint-spattered body parts. She cleaned herself up, ran a comb through her hair and then studied her reflection. She still looked youthful if she did say so herself. She'd never been vain and hadn't wasted much time fussing with her appearance, always believing that beauty came from within. Even so, she wondered what Josh thought about the way she looked.

"Stop it right there," she whispered to herself. Josh was a friend. Period and end of story. That was all he could be. Her focus needed to be on her girls and her business.

When she stepped back into the dining room, Josh was waiting by the door. He'd closed the cans of paint and had covered the rollers and paintbrushes in what looked like plastic wrap. He was cleaned up and his hair neatly brushed. Seeing how good he looked made her glad that she'd taken the time to repair her appearance.

"I'll drive," Josh said. "I have my work truck so a little paint on the seats won't hurt anything."

"I can't believe how much paint I got on myself."

"It happens." He opened the door for her and removed a clipboard from the passenger seat so she could sit. Although he'd described it as his work truck, it was clean.

Once he was behind the wheel, he turned on the truck and looked at her. "Where to?"

She named a deli a short distance away that she remembered had the best sandwiches and homemade salads. As a small business owner herself, she liked to support her neighbors in the community. She leaned back in the seat and lowered the window, letting the gentle breeze float over her. It blew her hair and she raised a hand and held it away from her face. "I'm not keeping you from working, am I?"

"What do you mean? You're the one who told me to take a break."

She shook her head. "You know what I mean. Other jobs. Paying jobs."

"Nah. I have a good team. Someone will call me if an issue arises."

"Sounds good. And let me know if something comes up and you have to leave."

"Nothing's going to come up."

They arrived at the deli and he parked. There were only a couple of people in line ahead of them, so they were able to get their sandwiches, salads, chips and drinks in under ten minutes. Tables and umbrellas were set up on a back patio, and they sat there. Kirby took a bite of her Reuben sandwich and closed her eyes. "This is so good. I can't remember the last time I came here for lunch."

"Why not?"

"Work. And the girls' activities. One of my friends gives them art lessons, which they love. And then there are dance lessons and sports."

"When do you have Kirby time?"

"Not often," she admitted. "Every once in a while I have girls' night out with friends, which is great."

"Being a single mom can't be easy."

"No. But I wouldn't trade my girls for the world."

"They are adorable."

"Lily couldn't stop talking about you."

"She's a charmer."

"That she is." Kirby deliberately didn't bring up Violet. She didn't want to tell Josh that her older daughter didn't like him. He'd already figured that out for himself.

They talked about everything and nothing while they ate, and Kirby laughed more than she had in ages. When they finished their lunches, they leaned back in their chairs and soaked up the sunshine and fresh air.

"I could get used to this," Kirby said, taking in

a deep breath and closing her eyes briefly. "But not today," she added, getting to her feet before Josh could volunteer to paint the coffee shop alone.

His cell phone rang as they were walking back to his truck. He looked at the caller ID and frowned before he answered the call. Although Kirby could only hear his side of the conversation, she had a feeling that something was wrong.

"What's the matter?" she asked when he ended the call.

"Looks like I spoke too soon earlier."

"Problem?"

"Yes. That was my plumber. He's run into an issue at a house we're renovating."

"Do you need to get over there? If so, you can drop me back at the coffee shop and I can continue painting." It wouldn't be as much fun without him, but she didn't want his kindness to interfere with his business. His paying jobs had to come first.

He paused as if considering his words. "Actually, the site isn't far from here. If you don't mind going with me, I can go handle the problem now. It shouldn't take long."

"I don't mind at all. You're the one doing me a favor. Besides, I really want to see some of your work."

"I'm not doing carpentry on this job. But if you're

up for a field trip in a few days, I can show you some of my work."

"I'd like that."

"Then it's a date."

Kirby's heart skipped a beat at the word *date*. Was it a date? Not necessarily. People used that word all the time. It just meant that they were agreeing to get together at a certain time so he could show her some of his carpentry. She was making way too much of that one simple word.

Josh turned a corner and drove another couple of blocks before he pulled in front of a large house. Several beat-up pickups lined the quiet street. The houses in this neighborhood sat on enormous tree-filled lots. Like so many others, this neighborhood was being gentrified. Kirby hated to see that charming features like built-in bookcases and stained-glass windows were regularly ripped out in favor of the modern look the design shows and magazines were featuring. To her, everything looked the same. Boring. Bland. Generic.

"Do you want me to wait in the truck?"

He looked surprised at the question. Before answering, he glanced at her from head to toe. His gaze left fire in its wake and she had to struggle not to squirm in her seat. "You're wearing enclosed shoes, so I don't have to worry about you cutting your foot or anything. You will need a hard hat, though. I have an extra in the back." He reached behind his seat and picked up a hard hat and set it on her head.

"Thanks."

They walked side by side up the wide, concrete stairs and onto a shady porch. She could picture a happy couple sitting together on a porch swing on cool evenings, talking quietly about their days. The porch was so big there was also enough room for a sitting area. She hoped the owners didn't do anything radical that would ruin the aesthetic.

Josh held the door for her and she smiled as she stepped inside and saw the dark woodwork and repaired plaster. She ran a hand over the paneling. "This is beautiful."

"I know. The owners are restoring this old girl to her former glory. We finished the front rooms a couple of days ago. Today we've run into a plumbing issue. I need to see how bad it is before talking with the owners."

She followed Josh to the kitchen, which had been ripped back to the studs. Two men were having a spirited discussion that included lots of waving arms and pointing. Josh approached them and joined the conversation. After a few minutes of more gesturing, he nodded and one man walked away. She couldn't tell if he was satisfied with Josh's answer or not.

Josh spoke to the remaining man and the two of them laughed together. Josh looked over at her and motioned for her to join them. Suddenly feeling self-conscious in her paint-spattered clothes and hard hat—she was the only person wearing one—she made her way over to them.

"I want you to meet someone," he said, holding out his arm to her. "This is my friend Eddie. He's also a recent transplant from Buffalo. This is Kirby, owner of Kirby's Perks and the maker of the best cappuccino outside of Italy."

"Nice to meet you," Eddie said with a smile.

"You, too."

"Well, we need to get back to the coffee shop," Josh said. "Call me if you run into anything else."

"Will do."

Instead of walking back through the house, Josh led Kirby out the back door. As they walked around the house, he stopped and inspected the masonry in a couple of places. The bricks all looked the same, so if repairs had been made, they were perfect. Josh must have been pleased by what he saw because he nodded to himself.

"All good?"

"Yes. My subcontractors always do good work, but I like to check, just to be sure. After all, at the end of the day, it's my name on the contract. My reputation is important to me. I don't want it ruined because of someone else's shoddy work. And that's especially important on this job because my family referred it to me. I definitely don't want anyone ruining their good names, either."

"As a business owner, I completely understand."

The return trip to the coffee shop was quick, and before long, they were back at work. Kirby had done physical work in the past, but her shoulders and arms were starting to ache. She had a feeling that when the painting was done, she was going to be in agony. But despite her aching muscles, she was enjoying herself.

"Tell me about yourself," she said to Josh.

"What do you want to know?"

She brushed the roller high up the wall and winced, immediately regretting the motion when pain shot through her shoulders and neck. She raised and lowered her shoulders and then tried to massage them as best she could.

"What's wrong?"

"I'm kind of feeling the effects of the painting."

The walls were tall, and even using an extension pole, she often had to reach way over her head. Especially when she'd tried to do some of the ceiling, which had been a huge mistake. She'd had to hold her neck and head at an odd angle, and after a few minutes, she'd given up and gone back to painting the walls.

"You know I can do this myself," he said.

"I do. But it's important to me that I help. I really can't explain why."

"So you probably wouldn't be too happy with me if I came back later tonight and finished on my own."

"That's putting it mildly. Although I appreciate the gesture, I need to be a part of this."

"I understand." He'd finished painting around the windows and trim and was now using a roller. He set it down in the tray and crossed the room. "But I can help you massage out some of those knots."

"That's not necessary." The idea of having his hands on her was at once tempting and nerve-wracking.

"I have magic hands."

Before she could object, he set his hands on her shoulders and began gently squeezing the tight muscles. It felt so good that any objection she would have made froze inside her. She lowered her head, giving him better access to her aching muscles. Though he was only trying to take the pain away, there was something sensual about his touch. Gradually he moved from her neck and shoulders and began working on her back, running his hands up and down her spine. It felt wonderful. And not just the way he was massaging the aches out of her muscles. It was being touched. By him. She moaned and bit her bottom lip to keep any more from breaking free.

Though she wanted him to continue, she forced herself to pull away and looked somewhere over his shoulder, being careful not to get too close. His touch had gone from being healing and soothing to being erotic. Arousing. Now she was filled with desire. "Thanks. I feel better now."

"Glad I could help." His voice was low. Husky. Tempting.

Neither of them moved and sexual tension arced between them. The longing simmering inside her was intense. She didn't know what to do now. How to get things back to normal between them. Whatever that might be. They hadn't known each other long enough to establish a baseline.

Josh must have been as befuddled as she felt, because he shook his head and blinked before he went back to the other side of the room and picked up his roller. She realized that he hadn't told her anything about himself, but she didn't trust herself to call him back over to resume the conversation, so she'd just have to be satisfied with what she knew about him. Although she didn't know him well, she had to admit that she liked what she did know. And that was a problem.

Josh forced himself to concentrate on his breathing as he returned to his side of the room. He hadn't intended to touch Kirby. That went against his plan of taking things slowly. Of being friends. But every moment they spent together made sticking to the playbook more difficult. She was just so beautiful his attraction grew the more time he spent with her.

When they'd driven to the deli for lunch, he'd had to force himself from staring at her sexy legs. They were so long and shapely his eyes were drawn to them over and over. Luckily she hadn't caught him looking. That would have been awkward. Being in those close quarters had been the sweetest torture. With each breath he inhaled, he got a whiff of her tantalizing scent.

As they'd talked, he'd gotten lost in the sound of her voice. Low and melodic, it was at once calming and arousing, which was a hell of a combination. He could have listened to her all day.

He'd enjoyed sitting outside with her during lunch, the wind tossing her black hair in the breeze. Truth be told, he enjoyed every second he spent in her company no matter what they were doing. When the opportunity to actually touch her presented itself, there was no way he could resist—especially when she gave herself over to the moment. Her skin was so soft it felt like heaven. As he'd massaged the knots from her muscles and felt her relax beneath his touch, he'd longed to spin her around and hold her in his arms. The desire to kiss her had nearly overwhelmed him. But that would have been a colossal mistake. She might have responded now, but he knew that she would regret it later. No, he needed to stick with the plan. No matter how much it pained him.

Besides, kissing Kirby was something the old, impetuous, "lead with his heart and not with his head" Josh would have done. The new and improved Josh was taking things slowly. There would be no more leaping before he looked, which always ended up with him trying to put together the pieces of his broken heart. The goal was to avoid heartbreak altogether. Which meant he and Kirby would be friends. Just friends.

After another hour, the alarm Kirby had set on her phone went off. She needed to get home and get cleaned up and then pick up her daughters from school. She placed her roller in the tray and then looked around. "You know, when you said it would take a couple days to get this done, I thought you were exaggerating. But now, I'm wondering if we'll get it done in time."

"Of course we will. Now, take a step back and look at your work. What do you think?"

She studied the walls she'd worked on and then turned to look at him. Her smile was bright and proud and he couldn't help but return it. "I like it. It looks so fresh and clean. When I look at the untouched walls, they look so dingy. I wonder why I never noticed before."

"They were fine. This is just better. When we're done you'll be ready for a grand reopening."

"After being closed for two days? I don't think that's necessary."

"Maybe not. But I know your regulars will be glad to be back. I've only had your cappuccino a few times, and I'm already experiencing withdrawals. I can't imagine how much they're suffering."

Kirby laughed and her brown eyes lit up. His heart skipped a beat and the blood began pulsing in his veins. There was no sense in denying it. He was seriously attracted to her. "I'm sure you'll all be fine. But I'd better get busy cleaning up here or I won't have a chance to change before I pick up the girls."

"I'll take care of everything here."

"I want to do my part."

"You're pretty stubborn, you know that?"

"So I've been told."

"And you don't like depending on people."

"That's not true. I know that everyone needs help now and then. But I don't ask people to do things that I can do myself. I don't want to take advantage of anyone."

He didn't consider himself just anyone, but perhaps she did. "I understand. But in this case, I'm not sure you can do this job as well as I can. So let me take care of the cleanup."

She stared at him as if trying to decide whether to accept his offer. Finally she nodded.

"Thank you so much. I guess I'll see you here same time tomorrow."

"I'll be here." Nothing could keep him away.

After packing up the coffee shop, he made a quick trip home, where he cleaned the rollers and brushes so they would be dry and ready in the morning. He'd taken a quick shower and was looking in the fridge for something to make for dinner when his phone rang. He checked the caller ID and smiled as he answered.

"Brian, what's up?"

"I'm calling to see what you're doing for dinner tonight."

"Coming to your place?" Josh said hopefully. Brian had gotten married recently to a wonderful woman, and they were parents of an infant daughter, Allie. Emmaline was not only a sweet woman, she was a great cook.

"Yep. That was an invitation. Emmaline made a roast, and since it's big enough for three, she suggested I invite my poor single brother so he won't have to subsist on peanut butter sandwiches."

"That's not what I said," Emmaline said loudly. Clearly she was nearby and could hear the conversation.

A moment later, his sister-in-law's voice came

over the phone. "That's not at all how the conversation went, Josh. I know you're new to town and a bachelor, and I figure you might want a home-cooked meal."

"I'd love one. I'm on my way. Thanks."

He lived near Brian, so it didn't take long for him to arrive. The delicious aroma of dinner greeted him the minute he stepped inside.

"Come on in," Emmaline said. "We were just putting food on the table."

"Need help?"

"No. We're all done."

Josh followed Emmaline into the kitchen. Dinner was a lively affair and Josh was glad to see his brother so happy. Brian had always been quiet and thoughtful. And Josh had been sure he hadn't wanted to get married or have children. Just look at him now.

After dinner, Emmaline rose. "If you gentlemen would excuse me, I want to do a bit of research while Allie is sleeping. It was good to see you, Josh. Feel free to stop by anytime."

"Thank you," Josh said as Emmaline left.

"But call first," Brian joked. "We're newlyweds after all."

"I know. Which is unbelievable considering how you were so sure you didn't want to get married."

"Yup, but that was before I kissed Emmaline. After that, I was a goner. It was only a matter of time before we got married." Brian grabbed the coffeepot. "Want more?"

Josh nodded. After taking one sip, he immediately thought of Kirby. "So, I'm doing some work at Kirby's Perks."

"The coffee shop?"

Josh nodded.

"What kind of work? I was there not too long ago and the place looked fine to me." He lifted his cup.

"Her roof was leaking, and I repaired it. And now I'm helping her paint."

"Painting? Since when do carpenters paint?" Brian set his coffee cup on the table without drinking. "Oh, no. Don't tell me."

"Don't tell you what?"

"You think you're in love with Kirby."

"I don't think I'm in love with her. I just met her."

"Since when has that stopped you?" Brian shook his head. "You are so predictable. You fall in love at the drop of a hat. When are you ever going to learn?"

Dinner had been delicious, but now Josh had a bitter taste in his mouth. He was starting to regret accepting the invitation. "Learn what?"

"You fall in love too fast. First there was Lynnette. You were so sure you were going to marry her."

"I was a senior in high school. Surely you aren't going to throw things I did as a teenager in my face."

"Fair enough. But what about Molly? Remember how you were ready to give up everything just to be with her?"

"I wouldn't go that far."

"You were going to close your company and move to Spain. Only to find out that she had a boyfriend over there that she hadn't mentioned to you."

"Well—"

"And don't forget Jennifer. You were so in love and she was just looking for someone to finish her kitchen for her. For free. And Allison, the woman you thought was the one."

Allison Smythe was the reason he'd left his life in Buffalo and moved to Rambling Rose. He'd been in love and ready to propose. He'd been crushed to discover that she'd been using him as a stepping-stone to someone with more money and contacts. "Feel free to stop anytime."

"I'm just trying to make a point. You fall too hard and too fast. I don't want you to do the same with Kirby. She's nice and I know she's not the type of woman to use you. But still. Slow down."

"It may surprise you, but I've already reached the same conclusion. I'm not the Josh who gets his heart stomped on and handed back to him. And Kirby really is just a friend."

"Good to hear it," Brian said. "Good to hear it."

Josh nodded. At least one of them was completely happy with that decision.

* * *

Kirby was at the shop when he arrived the next morning. She'd already opened the windows, airing out the place. The sweet aroma of coffee greeted him when he stepped inside, and he let out a small whoop.

Kirby looked at him and smiled. "I thought you might like a cappuccino before we get started."

"You read my mind." He placed the brushes and rollers on a drop cloth and then jogged across the room and took the cup from her outstretched hand. He took a sip. Delicious. "Perfect. That's heaven in a mug. You have got to teach me how to use that machine."

"It's easier than it looks." She lifted her own cup to her mouth. He tried not to stare at her full lips, but he failed. Some things were too beautiful to ignore. But when she caught him looking, he raised his own mug and took another swallow.

"I don't know about that, but I'm willing to let you tutor me."

She grinned at him and then finished her drink. Even though he could think of nothing more enjoyable than staring at her for the next few hours, he knew they had to get started if they were going to stay on schedule. He finished his drink and set the cup on the counter. He poured paint into a plastic tray liner and then handed it to Kirby.

"Do you want to put on your playlist or do you want to hear one of mine?" she asked as she took it.

He grinned and pulled his phone out of his pocket, set it on the counter and then turned to her. "I actually have a new playlist that I put together last night. I call it music to paint by." The playlist was a mix of the artists they both liked as well as others with similar styles.

They had been painting for about ten minutes when she called his name. "This music is great."

"I was hoping you would like it." He was also hoping that one of the songs would make her feel like dancing. It would really make his day if the mood struck her on a slow song so that he would have the opportunity to take her in his arms and hold her against his body. Of course, watching her shake and shimmy to a fast song would be good, too.

"I do." She dipped her roller back into the paint and turned back to the wall. He bit back a sigh and resumed painting. They were making good progress. If they were able to stick to his schedule, they would complete this room today. She'd painted a small part of the ceiling yesterday but had soon realized that the task was too difficult for a novice like her. Today he tackled that job while she painted the area behind the counter. Every once in a while he looked in that direction, just to get a glimpse of her.

Although she wasn't wearing makeup and her

T-shirt and cutoffs were casual, she looked exquisite. But her beauty wasn't limited to her looks. Her kindness and gentle spirit were just as gorgeous.

He hummed along to the music as he worked and before he knew it, it was time for lunch. They'd ordered a pizza, so he hopped in his truck and went to get it. On his way back to the coffee shop, he passed Petunia's Posies. Without thinking, he stopped to get some flowers for Kirby.

Wandering around the florist's, he tried to find just the right ones. A dozen roses was out of the question—they would be too romantic—but a bouquet of wildflowers should be acceptable. Finally he picked out an arrangement of purple and red flowers in a cut glass vase. Kirby seemed to like purple. Once he'd paid for them, he jumped back into his truck and returned to the coffee shop.

"Hey," he called as he stepped inside.

"I'm in my office," Kirby called. "Come on back."

Juggling the pizza and the flowers, he walked through the narrow hallway to Kirby's office.

Kirby's back was to him as she set paper plates and napkins on the table. "Times like this I'm envious of the businesses that have outside dining instead of a parking lot. Then we could dine alfresco instead of in my closet-sized office."

"I don't mind," Josh replied. He liked the intimacy. The office, though small, was well organized.

There was a three-drawer file cabinet in one corner with an overflowing basket of toys beside it. An open shelf held puzzles and board games. The desk was neat and there was a small table near the window, two folding chairs set across from each other.

She looked up. When she spotted the flowers, her eyes sparkled and she smiled. "How beautiful."

"I thought we might use them to fancy up the place."

"Good idea."

While he'd been gone, she'd washed up. Her hands were spotless, which, given the amount of paint that had been on them earlier, was nothing short of miraculous. She'd freed her hair from her ponytail and it now floated around her shoulders. She was nothing short of glorious.

"Let me go and wash my hands," he said, setting the pizza and vase on the table and dashing down the hall to the men's room. Once there, he washed up and then ran a comb through his hair. He frowned. He could definitely use a trim. Working as many hours as he did, he didn't visit the barber often and consequently he was looking a bit shaggy. That hadn't bothered him in the past. As long as he'd showered and his clothes were clean, he'd felt ready for the world. Now? Not so much. Now there was a beautiful woman to impress. There was nothing he could do about it today, but he was getting his hair cut before the week was out.

"I was beginning to wonder if I was going to have to eat the pizza all by myself," Kirby joked when he stepped back inside the office.

"Not a chance. It smelled so good that I almost pulled over and ate it before I got here." He placed two large slices on his plate.

"I would have been so mad." Kirby bit into her slice, closed her eyes and moaned softly. "That is so good. If I didn't have two growing kids who need to eat a balanced diet, I would live on pizza."

And he could live off watching her eat it. "Especially when it's this good."

He lifted his soda to his mouth and drank deeply, hoping the cold drink would cool him off. The way her tongue slipped out to corral the oozing cheese was doing things to his body that made him appreciate having the table between them.

All too soon the pizza box was empty and it was time to get back to work. There wasn't much painting left to do and he expected them to finish today. They'd made good progress and all that remained were the restrooms and the cleanup, which he didn't expect to take more than a couple of hours.

The restrooms were across from each other, and they kept the doors open so they could talk while they painted. He finished the men's room and went to help her with the slightly larger ladies' room. He'd insisted on painting the ceilings, so after they finished the walls, she left him to it.

"Is it okay to take the tape off the trim in the other room?"

"Sure."

He made quick work of the ceiling and then returned to the main area of the coffee shop. Kirby was kneeling on the floor, her back to him as she pulled on the blue painter's tape. A piece about two feet away from her stuck to the trim and as she leaned over to release it, he got an unobstructed view of her shapely bottom. He managed to smother the groan mere seconds before it escaped his lips. Not wanting to be a Peeping Tom or whatever you called a guy who stared at a woman's backside even though they were just friends, he took a few steps back, then called out to her as he walked into the room.

"Hey, I'm finished in the bathrooms."

She turned and smiled at him. "Great. I'm nearly finished in here. It looks great, doesn't it?"

"That it does. You're practically a pro. If ever I need a painter for one of my jobs, I know who to call."

She snorted a laugh. "Don't count on it. I think I'll stick to my day job."

"Don't say no so fast." He grinned. "Take a moment to think about it."

"After the way my shoulders and back ached last night, no thought is necessary. But if you and your crew ever need coffee, I'm your girl. And of course, it'll be on the house."

He liked thinking of her as his girl. He forced that thought away. She wasn't his girl. She was his friend. How many times did he have to tell himself to stop jumping into the deep end before it stuck? "That's a deal. You know I can't say no to your coffee."

They finished the cleanup, tossing the tape and plastic tray liners into the trash. Kirby insisted on folding the drop cloths neatly, so while she did that, he loaded the ladders and other assorted odds and ends into the bed of his truck. When that was done, they set the tables and chairs back in the dining room and cleaned the glass on the display counter.

When they were finished, Kirby looked around and smiled radiantly. "It looks brand-new. Thank you so much."

"You're welcome."

Before he knew what she planned, Kirby stood on tiptoe and kissed his cheek. Her lips were soft and warm and electricity shot through his body. He curled his fingers into his palms in order to keep from pulling her into his arms and kissing her for all he was worth.

"See you around," she said, and then, after locking the door behind them, crossed the parking lot and got into her car.

With a wave, she was gone, leaving him longing.

Chapter Six

Kirby added more hot water to her lukewarm bath and then leaned back in her clawfoot tub. Sighing deeply, she closed her eyes and sank down until she was submerged to her shoulders. Hours had passed since she'd impulsively kissed Josh, yet she couldn't keep her mind from replaying it over and over. She'd thought about it as she'd driven to pick up the girls from school, again while she'd served them dinner, and yet again while she'd read their bedtime stories and listened to their prayers.

Now alone in her bathroom, she relived the glorious moment her lips had brushed against his cheek. His facial hair had tickled and heat had rushed throughout her body. Even now, hours later, just thinking of that brief kiss sent tingles dancing down her spine.

She got out of the tub, dried off, smoothed lotion over her skin and then pulled on a pair of cotton pajama shorts and a tank top. She checked on the girls and then returned to her bedroom. The bath had loosened her tight neck and shoulder muscles some, but they still hurt a little bit. Nothing had felt as good as Josh's fingers as he'd massaged her yesterday. She'd hoped for a repeat today, but he hadn't offered and she didn't want to ask. That would have been too forward, and she hadn't known how he would have responded.

She checked the time. It wasn't too late. Hopefully Ginny was awake.

"I hope I didn't disturb you," Kirby said after her friend answered the phone.

"Nope. What's up?"

"Oh, nothing." Now that she had her best friend on the line, she had to find a way to discuss Josh.

Ginny laughed. "Really? So that's what we're going with? I've known you long enough to know that something is on your mind."

"Okay." Kirby blew out a breath. "I met a guy."

"Really?" Ginny's voice was intrigued.

"Yes. And I don't know what to do."

"Tell me everything."

"There's not much to tell. His name is Josh Fortune and he's a carpenter and contractor."

Ginny laughed. "Those Fortunes are getting around."

"Tell me about it." Ginny had recently become engaged to Draper Fortune, Josh's cousin.

"So, what's the problem?"

"Where to start? He's young. And carefree. And I'm a single mother of two."

"Which he knows?"

"Yes. And though Lily likes Josh, Violet has taken an instant dislike to him."

"Well, he is the first man since Will to be in your life, so that's not entirely unexpected."

"True." Kirby knew that, but hearing it from Ginny somehow helped.

"How did you meet?"

"The roof at the coffee shop was leaking and he fixed it for me. We repainted it."

"I see."

Kirby realized she'd been beating around the bush. And she also knew that Ginny would allow her to do that as long as she needed to. "I kissed him."

There was a slight pause. "And how did it feel?"

"Wonderful. Great. Terrible. Confusing."

"Sounds like."

"It was just a peck on the cheek to thank him for everything he's done for me."

"It must have felt like more than a peck if you're still thinking about it."

"None of this makes sense," Kirby said. "I'm a grown woman, not a teenager. So why am I thinking about a kiss as if it had been my first?"

"It was your first with Josh."

"True. But it was still just a kiss. I've been married and have two children. One kiss shouldn't rock my world like this."

"So, he rocked your world."

Kirby giggled. "Like you can't imagine. That's all I've been able to think about all day. I need to get my head back in the game."

"Did the girls notice that you were distracted?"

"No. They were so busy talking about their day at school and the assembly they had that they didn't notice how distracted I was. But I can't do that again. They need me to be present in their lives. I can't float around on clouds daydreaming about a man who's all wrong for me."

"Who said he's all wrong for you?"

"I do. He's too young."

"I think you're jumping to conclusions here. Before you decide he's not the man for you, take the time to get to know him. You might be pleasantly surprised."

"I'll try," Kirby said. They chatted a few more minutes about Ginny and Draper before ending the call.

She took a painkiller and then climbed into bed

and picked up the romance she was reading. Before Will's death, she hadn't read much in the genre, preferring mysteries. After his death, she couldn't focus enough to read at all. Once she'd gotten past the worst of her grief, she'd needed joy and happiness in her life. Books where a happy ending was guaranteed provided a sliver of that elusive happiness. There might not be a special someone in her life, but she enjoyed watching as two people fell in love and reached their happily-ever-after. And when she finished a book, she was assured that the main characters would live long, happy lives together. Something she and Will had been denied.

Tonight, she found her mind wandering and she couldn't concentrate on the relationship developing between the main characters. Instead, she found herself wondering if there might be a relationship developing between her and Josh. Was he the forever type? And why did it even matter? He was too young and she was too busy. The best thing was for the two of them to be friends. Surely she could be happy with that.

Setting down her book, she turned off the lamp. Since she couldn't read, she might as well make an early night of it. Tomorrow would be here before she knew it and she wanted to be alert. The coffee shop would be open tomorrow and she imagined all of her regulars would be there, not just for their usual beverages, but also to check out the changes.

When Kirby arrived at the shop the next morning, she was pleased to find that it was hopping. She put her purse in her office and grabbed her apron from its hook.

"This is busier than I expected," she said to Hillary as she joined her behind the counter.

"This is nothing. You should have been here half an hour ago for the grand reopening. You would think we were giving away money."

"Grand reopening? We were only closed for a couple of days." Kirby beckoned for the next person in line to come over. While she filled orders, she spoke to customers who told her they liked the look of the place. The general consensus was that the new color gave the coffee shop a modern look without losing its cozy feel.

Once things slowed down, she went around the room, spending time with each of her regulars. Rebecca looked at her ruefully as she held out her cup for a refill. "I'm so far behind on my writing. I tried to write at home and then at the library, but it didn't work. I need this environment and your coffee in order to function. Please tell me you aren't closing again in the near future. Or at least not until I turn in my book to my editor."

Kirby smiled. She didn't quite understand authors and their routines, but she respected the work. Rebecca wrote amazing thrillers and Kirby was a big fan. Her books were the one exception to the nothing-but-romance rule. "I can honestly say I have no plans to close anytime soon. Your deadline is safe with me."

"Thank goodness."

Kirby nodded and then wandered away so Rebecca could get back to work. Seeing Martin, Kirby went over and sat down across from him.

"What do you think about the changes?" she asked.

"I like them. They're nice. But there's something to be said about not wiping out the past."

"I know what you mean. There have been a lot of changes in Rambling Rose over the past decade or so."

"Yes. I see the changes that the Fortunes have made. They've definitely made their mark on this town."

Kirby couldn't tell whether he thought the changes were good or bad. Perhaps he believed they were both. And there was something about the way he'd said the name Fortune that gave her pause. But he didn't say anything further, instead asking her about her children.

They chatted for a few more minutes and then she

moved on. She had just finished making the rounds when the bell over the door chimed. The hair on the back of her neck rose a little and her skin began to tingle. Without seeing him, Kirby knew that Josh had just entered the shop. There was something about him that reached out and touched her on an elemental level. Whether that would ultimately prove good or bad had yet to be determined.

Turning, she smiled and approached him. “Coming to check out your work again?”

“Nah. I know we did a good job. I came to get my cappuccino fix.”

“Coming right up. If you want to sit down, I can bring it to you.”

He shook his head as they walked to the counter. “No. I want to watch you work that little machine so I can figure out just what I did wrong.”

“Ah, the truth is revealed,” she teased. “Your ego won’t let a simple machine get the best of you. Especially when I can practically work it with my eyes closed.”

“You know me all too well. Not the part about me worrying that you’re better at it than I am. You should be. It’s just that the machine seemed to be taunting me the other day.”

“Taunting you? You mean like laughing every time you pushed the wrong button? Hmm. I think you’re taking this a little bit too seriously.”

"You wouldn't be saying that if you heard the sounds it was making."

"I did hear them. There was grinding and groaning and an occasional scream. The screams were from you, not the machine."

He threw back his head and laughed. "You're a real regular comedienne, you know that?"

"Thank you very much," she said, doing her best Elvis impersonation. "I'm here all week. Seriously, the machine made sounds I'd never heard before. I'm surprised that it still works."

"I didn't break it, did I?" Josh sounded worried.

"No. It works the same as it did before." She flashed him a cheeky grin. "Of course, now it compliments me on every cappuccino I make and begs me never to go away again. That's new."

He laughed. "You're making fun of me."

"You know it." She handed him his drink. "How about something to eat with that?"

"Nah. I've got to run. I just came to get my fix." He took a swallow of coffee but didn't leave.

"Is there something else?"

"Actually, yes. I was wondering if you would like to go to dinner with me."

She hesitated. "That's nice of you to ask, Josh, but...well, I don't date. My life is complicated. You've seen that firsthand, so I don't need to explain."

"I'm not suggesting anything difficult. What I'm

proposing is actually pretty easy. Just dinner. Tonight."

"I would have to get a sitter. That won't be easy on short notice. I—"

"Kirby, I'm sorry I didn't make it clear but the girls were included in the invitation."

That comment pulled her up short and stifled whatever objection she was about to utter. Then she recovered. "Really?"

He nodded. For a minute, Kirby tried hard to think of an excuse to say no. But then she realized she didn't want to. She liked Josh and enjoyed spending time with him. And dinner did sound like fun. Having her daughters along would keep each of them from getting the wrong idea.

"Okay, then. The girls and I would love to have dinner with you."

"Great. Give me your address. I'll pick you ladies up at five thirty."

"Sounds good."

Kirby watched as Josh walked away, whistling a jaunty tune as he went. She wasn't sure what had made her say yes, but she knew that she'd taken a step out of the past and into the present. Hopefully it was the right move for her.

Josh paused before ringing Kirby's doorbell. He looked at the gift bags and wondered if he was going overboard. But this was a first date, one that he hoped would lead to many more. He wouldn't get a second chance to get off on the right foot. Better to overdo it than underdo it. He rang the bell and hoped for the best.

"Somebody is at the door." Lily's young voice floated through an open window. "Can I look out and see who it is? I promise not to open it."

The voice was followed by the sound of little feet pounding on the floor. A moment later, the curtain on the glass front door moved and he saw two pretty young faces staring up at him.

"It's Josh," Lily said, smiling. She clapped her hands, clearly pleased to see him.

"I told you he was coming over to take us all to dinner." Kirby's face appeared and then the curtain dropped, and the door swung open. "Welcome. Come on in."

"Thank you."

"What's in the bags?" Lily asked.

"Gifts for you and Violet." He handed a bag to Lily and the other to Violet. He glanced at Kirby. "I hope it's all right. I probably should have asked first, but I didn't want to show up empty-handed for our first date."

"It's fine." She looked at her daughters, who were pulling the pink tissue paper out of their bags and setting it on the coffee table. "What do you say, girls?"

"Thank you," they replied in unison without looking up.

"You're welcome."

"It's a Barbie doll," Violet exclaimed, grinning broadly. "It's the one that I wanted."

Josh smiled. That day at the coffee shop he'd heard the girls talking about the dolls they liked and wanted. It seemed he had to go to every store in Rambling Rose to find the right ones.

"I got one, too," Lily exclaimed, holding the doll against her chest. "I love her so much. I'm going to name her Lily."

"That's a great name," Josh said.

"It's my name," she said seriously.

"I know."

"Wait a minute. I have a first-date gift for you, too, Kirby," Josh said. He pulled a wrapped box from behind his back.

Kirby smiled. "You didn't have to get me anything."

"Of course I did. It's our first date."

"But you already gave me flowers."

"Those were for the coffee shop. This is for you."

"All right."

"What did he give you?" Violet asked as Kirby began unwrapping the box.

"I don't know," Kirby said. Violet and Lily secured their dolls under their arms and then helped pull the decorative wrapping paper from the box.

"It's candy," Lily said.

Kirby smiled at him. "Thank you."

"You're welcome."

"What kind is it?" Lily asked.

"Chocolate," Kirby said. "My favorite."

"Can we have some now?" Violet asked.

"Not now. We're going to the restaurant for dinner, so let's put the dolls away and get ready to go. You can play with them when we get home."

Lily and Violet laid their dolls on the couch and then covered them with the previously discarded tissue paper so they could nap until the girls got back from dinner. They kissed the dolls and told them to have sweet dreams.

Although the girls seemed pleased with their gifts, Josh was still a bit nervous about the rest of the evening. He'd never dated a single mother before, but he knew it wasn't all smiles and laughter. Heck, he was surprised that Violet had been pleasant to him. But then, the night was still young. Her pleasure with the doll could wear off and once more she could become cool to him.

Since the girls needed their booster seats, they decided to take Kirby's car.

"Where to?" she asked when everyone was securely seat-belted.

"Roja. It's located in the Hotel Fortune."

"Really? Isn't that a bit…ritzy?"

He nodded. "Yes." He'd wanted to make a good impression. What better way than to go to one of the best restaurants in Rambling Rose?

"All right. But remember my girls are five and seven."

"I know." The restaurant was beautiful and he knew the girls would be impressed by how pretty it was. More than that, Kirby would be impressed.

As Kirby drove to the restaurant, the girls peppered them with questions. Violet had been cool to him the first time they'd met, but she'd warmed up to him a little. She even laughed at a couple of his really bad jokes. Of course he'd tried them out on Toby and Tyler, who'd found them hilarious.

Once they reached the hotel, they parked and went inside. Lily grabbed his hand and grinned up at him. "I have never been in this building before. It's big."

"The sign outside said Fortune," Violet said. "And that's your name. Is this your building?"

"No. But my cousins are the owners. And my brother Brady works here. He's the concierge."

"He's the what?" Violet's brow wrinkled in confusion.

"Concierge. He helps people who stay at the hotel."

"Helps them do what?"

"Oh, if they need reservations at a restaurant or

want tickets to a play in Austin, he helps make that happen."

"That's nice. It's good to help people."

"Yes, it is."

Josh approached the front desk and asked for his brother. Before long, Brady arrived. They greeted each other and then Josh introduced him to Kirby.

"It's very nice to meet you, Kirby," Brady said with a friendly smile. "And who are these two lovely little girls?"

"I'm Violet and this is my sister, Lily."

"Pleased to meet you," Brady said. He shook each of their hands and they giggled.

"Do you have a few minutes to join us?" Josh asked as they walked to their table.

"I guess I can stay for a little while. If I won't be intruding."

"You won't be," Kirby assured him.

They had just taken their seats when Mariana, one of Roja's chefs, came rushing over. Josh had only lived in town for a short while, but it hadn't taken him long to discover that everyone in town loved her. She was carrying a sealed envelope and looked a bit nervous. She brushed a trembling hand over her bleached blond hair before tucking it behind her back. She greeted Kirby and the girls and then turned to Josh and Brady. "Do you guys have a minute? I need to talk to you about something."

"Of course." Josh stood and glanced over at Kirby. "Will you please excuse me? This won't take long."

"Sure. Do you want me to order for you?"

"No. I don't think I'll be gone that long." He glanced at Mariana, who nodded in agreement.

Josh, Brady and Mariana found a secluded seating area in the lobby where they wouldn't be disturbed.

Mariana clasped the envelope against her chest. She inhaled deeply and then blew out a wobbly breath. "These are the DNA results. Now that I have them, I'm a little bit scared to open them."

"What's the worst that could happen? Finding out that you're a Fortune and related to us or finding out that you aren't?" Josh asked.

Simplifying the situation seemed to settle her. "I like the idea of you guys being part of my family. And I have a great relationship with the rest of the Fortunes, so I know that they'll welcome me. I never knew my father and with my mother being deceased, it would be nice to have blood relations again. I miss having a family."

"Then rip open the envelope and read the results," Brady said.

Her hands shaking, Mariana opened the envelope and pulled out a sheet of paper. Josh and Brady exchanged glances while they waited for her to read the results. Josh hoped that they would be whatever Mariana wanted them to be.

After a moment Mariana looked up, her eyes filling with tears. Josh's heart broke for her. He was searching for words of comfort when she smiled broadly. "It's true! I'm a Fortune."

Josh and Brady jumped to their feet and hugged her.

"Welcome to the family," Brady said, and Josh echoed him.

Mariana gave them a watery smile. After a few moments, her smile faded as the gravity of the situation settled in. "Wow. I'm a Fortune."

"Now that you know, what are you going to do with the information? Brady and I won't say anything to anyone unless and until you're ready to tell people." Josh looked at his brother, who inclined his head as if to concur.

"Thank you. To be honest, I'm experiencing so many emotions right now I'm not sure how I feel. But I know that I'm not in a position to make any big decisions right now."

"Can you put your feelings into words?" Josh asked.

"Some of them." Mariana sighed. "I'm not sure if I'm happy to be connected to you and all of the other Fortunes."

"No?"

"Wait. That didn't come out right. I'm happy to be a member of the Fortune family. But I'm sad that

Treat Yourself to Free Books and Free Gifts.

Answer 4 fun questions and get rewarded.

We love to connect with our readers! Please tell us a little about you...

▶ DETACH AND MAIL CARD TODAY! ▶

1. I LOVE reading a good book.
2. I indulge and "treat" myself often.
3. I love getting FREE things.
4. Reading is one of my favorite activities.

TREAT YOURSELF • Pick your 2 Free Books...

Yes! Please send me my Free Books from each series I select and Free Mystery Gifts. I understand that I am under no obligation to buy anything, as explained on the back of this card.

Which do you prefer?

- ❑ **Harlequin® Special Edition** 235/335 HDL GRCC
- ❑ **Harlequin® Heartwarming™ Larger-Print** 161/361 HDL GRCC
- ❑ **Try Both** 235/335 & 161/361 HDL GRCN

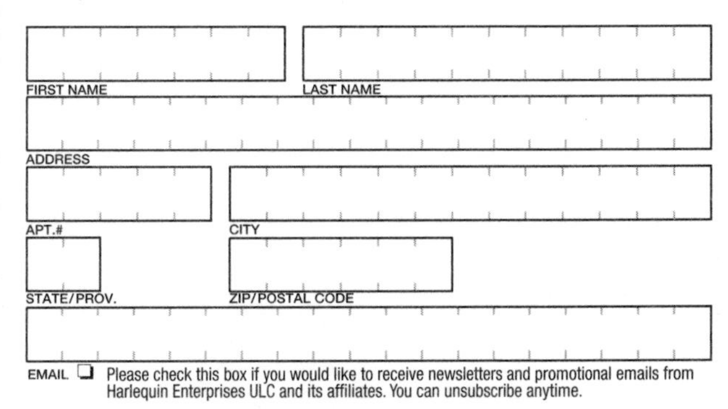
FIRST NAME
LAST NAME
ADDRESS
APT.#
CITY
STATE/PROV.
ZIP/POSTAL CODE

EMAIL ❑ Please check this box if you would like to receive newsletters and promotional emails from Harlequin Enterprises ULC and its affiliates. You can unsubscribe anytime.

Your Privacy – Your information is being collected by Harlequin Enterprises ULC, operating as Harlequin Reader Service. For a complete summary of the information we collect, how we use this information and to whom it is disclosed, please visit our privacy notice located at https://corporate.harlequin.com/privacy-notice. From time to time we may also exchange your personal information with reputable third parties. If you wish to opt out of this sharing of your personal information, please visit www.readerservice.com/consumerschoice or call 1-800-873-8635. **Notice to California Residents** – Under California law, you have specific rights to control and access your data. For more information on these rights and how to exercise them, visit https://corporate.harlequin.com/california-privacy.

SE/HW-820-TY22

my mother is gone. Now I might never learn the full truth from her about my heritage." She rubbed her forehead. "I guess right now I just need a minute alone to process my emotions."

"We understand." Brady and Josh each kissed her cheek and watched as she walked back to the kitchen.

"And I need to get back to work," Brady said. "I'll catch you later."

"Okay." Josh took two steps toward the restaurant.

"Hey," Brady called.

"Yeah?" Josh spun around.

"Kirby seems nice. And her girls are cuties."

"But?" Josh said. Because there always was a *but*.

"Take things slowly. You don't want to get ahead of yourself."

"What makes you think that's what I'm going to do?"

"That's what you always do."

"I'm not this time. This is a first date. A family date."

"And you chose Roja?"

"It's the best place in town."

"I know. I work here. But it's not exactly child friendly. I wouldn't bring the boys here."

"Lily and Violet are well-behaved. Not saying that Toby and Tyler aren't."

"I know what you meant so I'm not offended. I just hope you're right."

"I am."

"Okay. Enjoy your dinner."

"Thanks."

Josh returned to the table and then sat down besides Kirby. The girls were coloring the art page the restaurant provided to children. Violet was taking her time, carefully staying within the lines while Lily was using bigger strokes, often crossing over the lines.

"Is everything okay?" Kirby asked, setting her menu on the table.

"Yes. Mariana had some news she wanted to share with Brady and me. It's private, so I hope you understand."

"Of course. And I appreciate that you're keeping her confidence. Character counts, as I always tell my girls."

Character was something that was important to him, too. A woman could be rich or beautiful, but if she didn't have integrity, Josh wasn't interested in her company. From all he'd seen, Kirby had both beauty and integrity. As far as money went—well, wealth didn't matter to Josh. As long as he had enough money to provide for his needs, he was content.

His family had never been well to do. Then the recession of 2008 had hit, and things had gotten even worse for them. They'd fallen on hard times and had never quite recovered financially. When Josh had discovered that he had rich relations, he was happy to have more family. The fact that they were wealthy was irrelevant. His father had felt differently and still held a grudge against their wealthier relatives.

"We waited to order until you returned. If you want to look at the menu, I'll let the waitress know we're ready to order."

"Sure." He perused the menu. When the waitress returned, Kirby ordered for herself and the girls and then he placed his order.

"You want to hear something odd?" he asked when the waitress walked away.

"I wouldn't mind."

"Somebody has been sending presents to members of my family."

"What's odd about that?" Kirby asked.

"I like presents," Lily said, exchanging her green crayon for a blue one.

"Me, too," added Violet. "The Barbies were nice."

"I'll keep that in mind," Josh said.

Kirby shook her head. "You know you didn't have to bring them gifts."

"You're just jealous that I gave them dolls and all you got was a box of chocolates that you'll have to share."

She laughed. "You forgot about the flowers."

"No, I didn't." He would never forget the look of delight on her face when she'd spotted the bouquet.

Her eyes had lit up and her mouth had dropped into the cutest O before she gave a smile bright enough to illuminate all of Rambling Rose. "But remember, those were for the shop. Besides, I don't think the girls care much about sharing them."

"You're right." She took a sip of water. "But we're getting off track. Tell me about these gifts that your family members are getting."

"It started a few months ago. Several of my siblings and cousins got married in December. Five couples to be exact. A lot of family came in from out of town, including me, so we decided to have a Secret Santa gift exchange on Christmas Eve in the hotel ballroom so everyone could attend. Brady received an old bust of a horse's head. A plaque on it read, 'True beauty lies within.'"

"That's a lovely quote."

"I agree."

"Who was it from?"

"That's the strange part. No one knows. There wasn't a gift tag with it and no one admitted to giving it to him."

"Oh. That is weird."

"We all kind of laughed and didn't make a big deal out of it. But then my cousin Bella mentioned that she'd received a framed picture of a rose as a gift. It had the inscription, 'A rose by any other name would smell as sweet. MAF.'"

"MAF? What's that stand for?"

"Your guess is as good as ours. But those initials were also on a poem that my brother Brian found in a safe-deposit box."

"Do you remember the poem? That might be a clue."

"Yeah. It said something like this. 'What is mine is yours. What is yours is mines. I hope you can read between the lines. Love is forever, love never dies. You'll see it too, when you look in her eyes. MAF.'"

"Maybe this MAF is a poet although not a very good one."

Josh chuckled. "Maybe." Actually, he and his family wondered if the *MAF* was for Mary Ann Fortune, or Mariana, but since mentioning that might violate the other woman's privacy, he didn't share that bit of information. Kirby put her elbow on the table and leaned into her hand, clearly involved in the story. Her brown eyes sparkled with curiosity and her full lips parted in a small smile. "Then what happened? Has anyone else received an anonymous gift?"

"My cousin Beau received a little pink blanket."

"Like a baby blanket?"

He shrugged. "I guess. And my cousin Draper received a calypso record. But he doesn't have a record player, nor does he listen to calypso music."

"Wow. So what do you think it means?"

"I have no idea. Maybe it doesn't mean a thing."

"Oh, I love it all." She pressed her hands together

in obvious glee. "These are clues. You just have to figure out what they mean, who's sending them and why?"

"Oh, is that all?" He couldn't help but smile. Then he leaned in. "All right, Detective Harris. I'll put you on the case right now."

Kirby laughed. "I'll get right on it. I used to read mysteries all the time. More times than not, I figured it out before the big reveal. I'll have the case of the mysterious gifts solved in no time flat."

"Can I be your trusty assistant? Remember, I work for coffee."

"Ah. Then you're hired. When can you start?"

"Whenever you want me, I'm there. All you have to do is call and I'll do whatever you want or need me to do."

Kirby smiled as she watched the color crawl up Josh's neck and cheeks as he realized how suggestive his remark sounded. She knew he'd been joking, so she hadn't read anything into his words. Not wanting to make him even more uncomfortable, she let the moment pass without comment. Luckily the waitress brought their meals right then, and in the commotion of getting the girls' plates in front of them, enough time passed that changing the subject felt natural.

"What is this?" Violet asked, frowning at the food on her plate.

"It's chicken."

"It doesn't look like your chicken."

"It doesn't look like school chicken, either," Lily said.

Kirby glanced at Josh, who looked slightly alarmed. She'd tried to warn him that coming to such a fancy restaurant wasn't the best idea. Osteria Oliva, the casual Italian restaurant in the Shoppes, would have been a better choice. It was something a parent would know, but as a single man he clearly didn't. But they were here now and needed to make the best of it.

"What's the rule about new food?" Kirby asked.

"Give it a try before we decide we don't like it," Violet said glumly.

"And how many bites?" Kirby asked.

"Two bites to be sure," Lily said.

"But I already know I don't like it," Violet said. "It smells funny."

"Violet," Kirby warned.

Violet picked up her fork and then stared daggers at Josh as she brought the tiniest morsel of chicken to her mouth. There was no doubt that she blamed him for her current predicament.

"Well?" Lily asked in a small voice, her own fork hovering near her mouth.

Violet chewed and then answered, "It's not so bad,

I guess. It's not as good as Mommy's or chicken nuggets, but it's not nasty."

Lily took a taste and then gave a little smile. "I kinda like it. A little."

Josh looked up to the ceiling as if thanking his lucky stars and then started to eat.

"But I don't want to eat here again," Violet said, just in case she hadn't made her displeasure clear.

Kirby shot Josh a sympathetic look. He'd been so excited about tonight. Clearly the reality wasn't living up to what he'd pictured.

"I hear the desserts are good," Josh said, trying to salvage the evening.

"What do they have?" Lily asked.

"All kinds of cakes and pies. Ice cream, too." He hoped.

"I love cake," Violet said. "We should have it for dessert more instead of fruit."

"I'll think about it," Kirby said.

"It's almost my birthday," Lily said. "And we're having a princess cake."

"That sounds wonderful," Josh said. "Are you going to have a party?"

She nodded. "I'm going to invite my friends from school. But only the nice kids. I don't want any mean kids at my party."

Kirby's ears perked up. This was the first that she'd heard about mean kids. As far as she knew, all of the kids in Lily's kindergarten class were friends. Clearly that wasn't true. Perhaps the mean kids were the reason for Lily's unexplained stomachache.

Playing it casual, she took a bite of her steak before replying. "Who are the mean kids? I need their names, so I won't invite them to the party by mistake."

Lily shrugged and looked away.

"What do the mean kids do?" Kirby asked.

"I don't want to talk about it."

Kirby wanted to sigh in frustration but she held it back to probe further. "I can't help if you don't tell me who they are or what they do."

Lily shook her head and pushed her food around on the plate.

"So what do you want for your birthday?" Josh asked. Apparently he had reached the same conclusion that Kirby had. Lily wasn't ready to talk about the mean kids or what they did, and interrogating her would only make the situation worse. A wave of emotions crested over Kirby. As a mother, Kirby was furious that a child was being mean to her sweet daughter. Her mother's heart also broke with the knowledge that her child was hurting and she was powerless to make the situation better. She hated feeling helpless.

She'd felt the same way when Will lay dying in a hospital bed. If she could have, she would have infused him with life, but that was impossible. Besides, her husband hadn't given up on life. He'd wanted to live. Rather, life had been snatched from him by cancer and there was nothing anyone had been able to do to stop it.

Josh covered her hand with his and gave it a gentle squeeze. Perhaps he'd known how powerless she felt right now. She smiled at him, letting him know she appreciated his concern and valued his support. Although they were only friends, it felt good to know that she had someone in her corner right now. Of course, she wasn't truly without recourse. She intended to speak with Lily's teacher tomorrow. Maybe Mrs. Bennett would be able to identify the mean kids and find out what they had been doing to her little girl.

That resolved, Kirby pasted on a smile and resumed eating. After the awkward moment, conversation picked up although Violet only spoke to Josh if he asked her a direct question. She did laugh at a funny story he told, so that was progress, Kirby supposed. Once the bill was paid, they walked to the car.

"Can we go to the park?" Violet asked.

"Not tonight. It's getting dark."

"But we want to swing and play on the slide," she said.

"I'll take you to the park this weekend."

Violet frowned but she let the matter drop.

The drive home was quiet and passed quickly. When they walked up the porch stairs, Kirby's heart began to pound. The date was coming to an end. Would Josh attempt to kiss her good-night? And did she want him to? Of course she didn't. She hadn't kissed a man besides Will since she'd been a teenager. Even so, her heart was racing as she unlocked the front door and let the girls inside.

She turned to Josh, who was leaning against the front porch rail, looking like he didn't have a care in the world. "The girls and I had a good time tonight, Josh. Thank you."

He slowly crossed the floor until he was standing mere inches away from her. The heat from his body wrapped around her, raising goose bumps on her skin. She inhaled and got a tantalizing whiff of his cologne mixed with his own unique masculine scent.

"I had a great time, too. Maybe we can get together again soon."

"I'd like that."

"I'll call you."

"Okay."

He stepped back and turned to leave.

She fought the disappointment that filled her. Then he paused and turned back to her. In one movement he slowly lowered his head and she lifted her face to his. His lips brushed against hers gently and her knees nearly gave way. The feeling the simple touch aroused in her was almost her undoing. His lips captured hers again. The kiss lasted for mere seconds, but when it ended, Kirby was shaken to her core. Something inside her had shifted. Changed. She didn't know whether it was good or bad at this point, but she knew there was no pretending that Josh's kiss hadn't just rocked her world.

"See you later," he said, then jogged down the stairs as if the kiss had left him completely unfazed.

Did it mean nothing to him? Did he—

"Mommy," Lily called to her and Kirby shook herself out of her stupor. There would be time to ponder Josh's kiss and what it meant later. Right now her daughters needed her.

Chapter Seven

"What are we going to do now?" Lily asked Josh the following Saturday. She tapped her pink plastic hammer against her palm before placing it in the kid-sized tool belt he'd given her. He'd given a matching belt to Violet, but she wasn't interested in construction. Either that or she wasn't interested in him.

Josh had been spending quite a bit of time at the coffee shop completing odd jobs that Kirby hadn't gotten to, often with Lily by his side. Today he'd replaced a shelf in the storage room and put together a cabinet with Lily's "help."

"I don't know. We worked pretty hard today. I was

thinking that maybe we could get lunch and bring it back for Violet and your mom. What do you think?"

"And ice cream? Mom and Violet love ice cream." She flashed a charming smile and he laughed. She definitely had him wrapped around her little finger.

"Only your mom and Violet? I think you might like ice cream, too."

She nodded. "It's my favorite. And cake."

"We'll have to ask your mom about the dessert."

He put the hammer in his tool belt and then he and Lily walked down the narrow hall to the front of the coffee shop. Lily grabbed his hand and swung their arms back and forth. When he looked down at her, she gave him a snaggletoothed grin.

Kirby's Perks was busy this morning, but Kirby and Hillary were keeping things moving. Josh had been around often enough that he recognized many of the regular customers. There was the group of knitting ladies sitting around two tables they'd pushed together, and a couple of the Girl Scout moms grabbing coffees to go.

Josh could have watched Kirby all day. She was so graceful. Watching as she moved behind the counter was like watching a ballet. She didn't walk so much as she glided across the floor. And she treated her customers as if they were close friends or family, being gracious to the kind and grumpy alike. No wonder that her business was a huge success. People enjoyed basking in her presence, which was why there were very few vacant tables, even on a sunny and pleasantly mild day like today. Kirby closed the coffee shop at two o'clock on Saturdays and she didn't open at all on Sundays, so the customers needed to get their fix of her delicious brew now.

"Are we going to ask Mommy or not?" Lily asked, giving his hand a tug when he just stood there staring.

"Yep. Come on." As they walked up to the counter, he felt Violet's eyes on him. She'd said hello to him when he'd stepped into the shop, but that was the extent of their interaction. She was working on a crossword puzzle, and she turned her focus back to the book, nibbling on the pencil as she tried to find the right word. She was every bit the puzzle for him as the crossword was to her. One day she was happy to see him and treated him like a friend, sharing jokes that she'd learned at school. The next she was cool as if she realized she'd let him get a little too close. Clearly she hadn't decided what type of relationship they were going to have. He respected her right to her mixed feelings. After all, her mother seemed to be suffering from the same affliction.

One minute she was smiling at him. Even kissing him. The next he was firmly in the friend zone. Her inconsistency left him unsure which way to move. Being her friend was easy. They had a great time together. Waiting for her to see him as more than her friend—not so much. But he knew that she had a lot going on in her life. Being a single mom was a full-time job. Add to that being a businesswoman who was a huge part of the community, and she had a full plate. Even so, he wanted a definitive sign that she was interested in a romantic relationship. As the thought filled his mind, he heard Brian teasing him about always wanting to take his relationships to the next level too fast, even bringing out some of Josh's relationship greatest hits. He knew he needed to be patient and slow down.

"Josh wants to take me to get some ice cream. Do you want some?" Lily's words penetrated his mind and he realized that Kirby was looking at him.

"I want ice cream," Violet said, joining them at the counter.

"Whoa," Josh said, holding up his hand. "What I said was, Lily and I were going to run out and get lunch for the four of us. Then if you agreed, I would treat us all to ice cream. After lunch."

Lily asked, "Can we still get ice cream? Say yes, Mommy."

Kirby sighed. "I guess that would be okay."

"What are we getting for lunch?" Violet asked.

"I don't know," Josh said.

"Can we get hot dogs from the stand? Those are d-e-l-i-c-i-o-u-s."

"What does that spell?" Lily asked.

"Delicious," Violet said, with a proud grin.

"Yay!" Lily exclaimed, clapping her hands. "I like hot dogs. Especially the long pickle. It tastes so good."

He looked at Kirby. "I guess it's hot dogs."

"And chips," Violet said. "They have little bags for one person."

"Not like the big ones Mommy buys for us to share."

"I guess it's hot dogs and chips for the win," Kirby said. "To be honest, a hot dog does sound good."

"Then Lily and I will run out and be right back."

"I want to come, too," Violet said.

"And we want you to come," Josh added. He was relieved that Violet was once again receptive to him. Or maybe it was the hot dog. Either way, he'd take it.

The hot dog stand was only two blocks away, an easy walk for the girls. Lily still held his hand, and now she grabbed Violet's and the three of them started off down the street.

"Do you think Mommy will let us go to the park?" Lily asked Violet.

"I hope so."

"You girls really like going to the park," Josh said. "Do you meet your friends there?"

"Sometimes some kids we know come and we

play games," Violet said. "But mostly we like to play on the swings and the slide."

"I like the slide the best," Lily said. "They have a big twisty one, even bigger than on the playground at school."

"I like swinging really high and then bailing out," Violet said.

"I don't. I hurt my knees that time. I was bleeding and the school nurse put a Band-Aid on it. I didn't cry," she hastened to add in case anyone doubted her bravery. "And then I got a big scab, but Mommy said not to pick at it or it would get 'fected."

"*In*fected," Violet said. "And there is grass at the park, so if you land wrong it doesn't hurt."

"I still like the slide better," Lily said.

Josh listened as the sisters talked and an idea formed in his mind. He was familiar with their neighborhood. Although most of the houses were modest, the yards were quite large. He hadn't seen their backyard, but even a small yard would have enough room for him to build a play structure for the girls. That is if Kirby agreed.

There was no traffic when they reached the corner, so Josh ushered them into the street. But the girls wouldn't budge. They stood still and stared at him. Why were they looking at him? "There aren't any cars coming, so we can cross."

"Look to the left, look to the right, cross at the

corner, walk with the light," Lily and Violet chanted in unison as they stood there.

"Oh. Right," Josh said as if he did that all the time.

As the girls repeated the rhyme, they looked first to the left and then to the right. They were on a side street with only a stop sign and not a light. But he supposed it was all the same. "Ready now?"

After they crossed the street, they resumed their conversation about the park and the fun they had there. "There is a sandbox, but we don't play in it. That's for little kids," Lily said.

"Apart from the swing and slide, what else do you like to do at the park?"

"Run," Violet said. "I'm fast."

"I like to do cartwheels," Lily said. "We go to tumbling and ballet, you know."

He didn't know, but he nodded anyway.

When they reached the hot dog stand, the girls gave very extensive instructions on how they wanted their hot dogs prepared. Josh's and Kirby's orders were simpler. They wanted the works. The worker placed the hot dogs and chips into a paper bag and handed it to Josh.

"Can we carry our own chips?" Violet asked.

"Okay. But you have to hold hands and walk right beside me," Josh said. He fished out the chips and gave each girl a bag. This time when they got to the corner, he didn't make the same mistake. He knew better to wait for them to go through their rhyming routine.

When they returned to the coffee shop Josh blew out a long breath. The two-block walk had been unexpectedly intense. This was the first time Kirby had entrusted him with her precious children. Until right this minute, he hadn't realized what an awesome responsibility caring for them was.

"We're back," Violet exclaimed the minute they stepped inside.

Kirby looked up. "I see."

Business had slowed and only the regulars and a couple by the window were still there.

"Let's wash our hands and get our drinks," she told them. "Then we'll eat."

Josh set the food out on the table and was sitting down when the girls returned. Lily climbed on the bench next to him and gave him her brightest smile. As the girls sipped their juice pouches they told Kirby about things they'd seen on their walk to the hot dog stand. Birds splashing in a fountain. Butterflies flitting in the wildflowers in a planter outside a corner store. Funny, he'd passed those same things without giving them a second thought. Life was certainly full of wonders when you were a child who paid attention to every detail.

They were just finishing lunch when a woman came in. Kirby got up to help her while Josh and the girls gathered the trash. The regular customers had begun leaving one by one over the past twenty minutes, and the couple by the window had left, too. Now the shop was empty, and Kirby turned the Open sign to Closed. She filled a dishpan with disinfecting soap and water and began wiping the tables and chairs. He grabbed a broom and swept the floors before filling a bucket and grabbing a mop.

"You don't have to do that," Kirby said.

"I know. But many hands make light work."

"Suit yourself."

Working together, they managed to clean the coffee shop quickly. Once they were finished, Kirby set the alarm and they stepped outside.

"Can we go to the park?" Lily asked.

"Only for a little while. I have a lot of work to get finished at home."

"Do you mind if I tag along?" Josh asked. "I have something I want to discuss with you."

"That sounds ominous," Kirby said with a raised brow.

"It's not. It's actually something nice that I hope you'll agree to."

"In that case, you're more than welcome to join us."

Kirby and her girls got into their car and he followed them in his truck, parking beside them in the lot. The minute the girls were standing on the sidewalk, they dashed across the grass to the swings. Josh and Kirby followed more slowly.

"What did you want to talk about?" Kirby asked. She turned to look at him, using her hand to shade her eyes. The sun was high in the cloudless sky, but fortunately the day was still pleasant.

"On the way to get hot dogs, the girls mentioned how much they enjoy coming here."

"It's just about their favorite place in the world."

"I know you're busy and coming here takes time out of your day."

"My girls mean the world to me, so no sacrifice is too great."

He raised a hand to forestall her. The last thing he wanted to do was raise her hackles. "I know. You're a great mom. But I was wondering how you would feel if I built a swing set for them in your backyard. That way they could play on it whenever they wanted and you could get your housework done at the same time. It would be a win-win."

"That would be nice. I had considered it before but—"

"But what?" he urged when she didn't continue.

"When the girls were little, Will and I used to bring them to this park to play. We all had so much fun together. Lily was barely two, so I know she doesn't remember it. Violet was four when we lost

Will, so she might have some memories. Coming here together is a way to keep that tradition alive."

He didn't know what to say to that, so he was silent as they walked across the lawn to where the girls were playing. He should have known there was a connection to her husband and this park. Even though he had died years ago, he was still a huge part of everything Kirby did.

"But," Kirby said, bringing him to a halt, "it would be more convenient for me and a lot more fun for them if they had their own swing set. School ends in a few weeks, so they won't have recess and they'll lose that opportunity to swing and slide. Okay. Let's do it."

"I was hoping you would say that. When the girls are finished playing, we can stop by a store. If you see one you want, I'll load it in my pickup tonight."

"When will you be able to put it together?"

"Anytime."

"Don't you have to work?"

"I do. But my schedule is flexible. Besides, it will only take a few hours."

She reached out and touched his cheek. Her hand was soft and smelled vaguely of floral soap. It took all of his strength not to turn his face into her hand and kiss her palm. "You really are a nice man, Josh Fortune. I'm very glad you came into our lives."

That sounded as if she were slotting him in the

friend zone, but he smiled anyway. Good relationships were based upon friendship. And friends spent time together getting to know each other. That was never a bad thing.

And then there was that kiss. Although it had occurred days ago, his mouth still tingled at the memory. It had been fleeting, over nearly as soon as it had begun, but it had a lasting effect on him. The moment his lips had met hers, he'd felt as if he'd been struck by lightning. Nothing in his experience had prepared him for the physical and emotional impact that one little kiss had on him. Everything inside him had screamed for him to take her into his arms and deepen the kiss, but he'd resisted the impulse. He'd known instinctively that Kirby wasn't ready for anything more. And since that was the case, he was going to take things slowly. There was no way he wanted to get his heart broken again.

He doubted that she'd kissed another man since her husband's death. She was definitely cautious and he was in uncharted territory. With each moment they shared, his feelings for her grew. He didn't want to blow his chance with her by coming on too strong. Which was why he hadn't mentioned the kiss. Or another date. He wanted to take her out again, but next time he wanted it to be just the two of them. In the meantime, he was spending as much time with her as he could without making a pest of himself.

Which was why he'd been looking for projects to do around the shop. While he worked, he got the chance to be with her. A chance to make her laugh and watch as her eyes sparkled with mirth. A chance for her to see him as a man who could be more than a friend.

"I'm glad to have come into your life," he replied.

They reached the girls and Violet asked her mother to give her a big push.

Lily had been climbing the ladder on the slide, but when she saw Kirby push Violet, she slid down and ran over, her little legs moving quite fast for someone her age.

"Can you push me, too?" she asked, hopping onto a swing.

"How about I give you a push?" Josh said.

"Okay."

Kirby and Josh stood side by side, pushing the girls on the swings. Violet flew high in the air and then bailed out of her swing, soaring through the air before landing on her feet.

"I can't believe I used to do that as a child," Kirby said as Violet raced over and hopped on her swing again. "Now the very idea terrifies me."

"Oh, come on," Josh said. "You have to be braver than that."

"Do I?"

"Girls, your mom and I are going to swing, so can you pedal yourselves for a while?"

"Yep."

Josh grabbed Kirby's hand and led her to a vacant swing.

"I'll swing, but I'm not bailing out."

"Chicken," he said and then began squawking like a chicken.

Kirby laughed but Lily shook her head at him. "It's not nice to make fun of people. That's what the mean kids do."

Josh stopped teasing immediately and looked at Lily. "You're right. I shouldn't have teased your mother. I'm sorry, Kirby."

"Lily, you're right, it's not nice to make fun of people," Kirby added. "But I know Josh was just joking."

"You aren't sad that he called you a chicken?"

"Nope. Want to know why?"

Lily nodded.

"Because I am scared to jump out. And there's nothing wrong with that."

"Me, too. But Violet isn't scared."

"Violet's bigger than you are."

"You're bigger than Violet."

"True. But I'm still not going to bail out. I have fun just swinging."

"Me, too," Lily said.

"But if Josh and Violet want to bail out, good for them. I'll be happy for them. I might even clap."

"Me, too." Lily turned from her mother to look at Josh. "Are you going to bail out?"

"Yep." In a few pumps of his legs, he was swinging high in the air. Kirby and the girls stopped swinging while they watched him. When he was as high as he could get he let go of the chains and propelled himself through the air. That bottomless feeling hit his stomach and he flew for a moment before gravity claimed him, bringing him down to the ground.

"That was great," Lily said, clapping and running over to where he was still squatting.

"Thanks." He stood and turned. Kirby and Violet were also clapping and Violet even cheered.

"I never saw anybody go that high before," Lily said. "Even the big kids don't go that high."

"I'm bigger than they are."

Lily ran back to the swings but he went slower. He'd jarred himself on the landing and now his legs were a bit wobbly.

"Are you going to do that again?" Lily asked when he sat down beside her.

"Yes, Josh, are you going to do that again?" Kirby asked, smirking. No doubt she'd noticed the way he walked.

"No. I think I'll just swing for a while."

Kirby gave him a knowing look. "Scarier than you remember, huh?"

He laughed. "I'm no wuss, but I had to bite back a scream."

She threw her head back and laughed.

He'd been exaggerating, of course, but it was worth it to see Kirby enjoy herself even if it was at his expense.

"Everything is scarier when you realize what could go wrong," she said quietly.

"True. With two little girls, you must be afraid all the time."

She glanced at her daughters and his eyes followed her gaze. Violet was now swinging standing up and Lily was on her stomach. She'd turned in circles, twisting the chains. Now she lifted her feet and the swing was spinning rapidly in circles as the chains unwound. Just looking at her made him dizzy.

"I was for a while after Will died. He'd been young and healthy until then. Never had so much as a cold. He ate right. Exercised. Didn't drink or smoke. But somehow he ended up with liver cancer. After he died, I was scared. I watched the girls like a hawk. Every fever or cough sent me to the pediatrician in a panic. I'd lost my husband. I couldn't lose one of my girls. I was also worried about myself. What if I got sick? What would happen to my sweet babies? I knew my parents or my brother or sister would step in, and my in-laws, but that didn't keep my mind from considering every horrible thing that could go wrong."

"What changed?"

"I realized I couldn't go on like that. It wasn't healthy for me or the girls." As if worrying that she'd revealed more than she'd intended, she pushed off and began swinging, ending the conversation.

Her words stuck with Josh. He couldn't imagine living with that kind of worry. But then, hadn't he been stressed just walking with them two blocks? Parenthood was more than a notion, something he really hadn't understood before.

The four of them swung for a few more minutes before Kirby came to a stop and then stood. "Come on, girls, it's time to leave."

"Already?" Violet asked. "But we just got here."

"Can't we stay a little while longer?" Lily pleaded.

"Not today. We need to get going. We're going to a special store."

"What kind of store?" Lily asked.

"A store that sells swing sets. Josh is going to build one in our backyard so you'll be able to play at home when we can't come to the park."

Violet sailed her swing high in the air and then bailed out. The second she hit the ground she raced over to him. "Really and truly?"

The doubt that mingled with her joy hurt his feelings a bit. For some reason, Violet didn't trust him. "Really and truly."

She grinned and then she and Lily raced to the car.

"I guess a play structure is the way to their hearts," Kirby said with a grin.

"Yep."

They crossed the park and got into their vehicles. As he drove to the store, he wished he knew the way to Kirby's heart.

Chapter Eight

"Lily, I need you to come back over here with me," Kirby called for the umpteenth time. "If you keep getting in the way, we're going to have to go in the house."

"I'm helping Josh," Lily said. She put her hands on her hips and stomped her foot.

"Don't make me tell you again."

"Go sit with your mom and sister," Josh said, giving Lily a gentle pat on her back. Lily sighed and walked at a snail's pace across the lawn, and then with an exaggerated sigh, she plopped down on the blanket in the shade of the oak tree.

When they'd arrived at the store yesterday afternoon, the girls had gravitated toward the play structures designed for playgrounds. Kirby had preferred the smaller ones because as she said it would be easier for Josh to put together. He'd been offended. He was a carpenter, he'd told her, and could build a swing set in his sleep. Eventually they'd settled on a midsized set with all the bells and whistles. It had three swings, a long, twisting slide, a glider, a raised clubhouse, and a climbing wall that the girls had insisted they needed. Josh had loaded it into his truck and brought it to her house.

The girls had been too excited to go to sleep last night and they were up early this morning. They'd practically swallowed their breakfast whole, then sat on the front porch to wait for Josh. When he'd arrived, Lily had run down the stairs and greeted him with a hug. Violet wasn't as demonstrative, but she did at least follow her sister down the stairs.

Now they were sitting with Kirby under the tree in the far corner of the yard so they wouldn't get hurt. Violet was playing school with her dolls. Lily couldn't sit still for more than a few minutes before she was back wandering around the yard. Kirby didn't know if it was because she was excited to be getting a new swing set or because Josh was around and she adored him. Perhaps it was a combination of the two.

Finally Lily picked up the Barbie doll Josh had given her and began to brush the doll's hair. "I don't see why I can't help."

Kirby sighed. She and Josh had explained numerous times about how dangerous it was and how they didn't want her to get hurt. That hadn't done the trick, so this time Kirby tried another approach. "Because Josh can get it done faster on his own."

"You always say two people can do a job faster than one. And that three people can get it done faster than two when we help you."

"You do say that a lot," Violet added, looking up from the paper she was "grading." After adding her two cents she turned her attention back to her students, chastising them for talking the minute her back was turned.

"And most of the time it's true. But this is something Josh can do faster on his own. Just look at him," Kirby said, turning her attention to where Josh was fastening two long pieces of cedar together. Her eyes were drawn to his muscular torso. His chest and bicep muscles bulged as he turned the screwdriver. There wasn't a bit of fat on him and the blue T-shirt clung to his strong body and well-defined six-pack.

No wonder Lily kept straying to his side. That man was magnetic. Kirby felt the pull that kept drawing her to him. The sun was shining brightly, and although it was only midmorning, it was hotter than it had been the past few days. Josh wiped a bit of sweat from his brow and her fingers ached to push aside his hand and brush his damp hair from his forehead. To run over his strong back and shoulders and feel the muscles tensing beneath her hands. She curled her hands into fists on her lap instead. He must have felt her staring, because he looked up. When he caught her eye, he winked.

Flushing, she looked away. The last thing she needed was for him to know that she was fantasizing about him. Who knew where her mind and her body would lead her if she and Josh were alone? Suddenly thirsty and overheated, she stood. "I'm going to make a pitcher of lemonade. You girls stay on the blanket and away from Josh."

"We won't move a muscle," Violet said. She looked meaningfully at Lily.

"I won't move a muscle, either," Lily said reluctantly.

Kirby crossed the yard and went into the house. The second she was alone in the kitchen, she breathed out a pent-up sigh and leaned against the table. *Whew.* That man was doing things to her body that she hadn't expected. Feelings she'd thought were dead and buried were proving to be alive and well. Ordering herself to get a grip, she went to the window and looked out. The girls were still on the blanket as promised and Josh was hard at work and looking quite delicious. Kirby washed her hands and then grabbed the pitcher, lemons and sugar. She could make lemonade without thinking, which, given the way her mind kept wandering to Josh and how sexy he looked in his T-shirt and cargo shorts, was a good thing.

Although she and Josh were only friends, she'd taken special care with her appearance today. Apart from the time they'd gone to dinner when she'd worn a dress, he'd only seen her in jeans, T-shirts and an apron, or the old shorts she'd worn to paint. Today she'd put on a pretty summer dress that stopped a few inches above her knees, and a pair of flat sandals. Her hair was loose and free around her shoulders. She'd even dug around in her jewelry box until she found a pair of her favorite earrings and an ankle bracelet that she hadn't worn in quite some time. As she'd combed the girls' hair and added colorful bows and barrettes this morning, they'd said she looked pretty.

And she felt pretty. It had been a while since she'd put this much effort into her appearance just to sit around the house. She only wore makeup and jewelry on special occasions, and even then, the barest minimum. Professional manicures had long since gone out the window. But last night, after the girls had finally fallen asleep, she'd filed and polished her fingernails. They looked pretty good if she did say so herself. Although why she was going to so much trouble when there was absolutely nothing going on between her and Josh was a mystery to her.

She paused the wooden spoon midstir. Who was

she trying to kid? There was no mystery why she was suddenly interested in her appearance. She was attracted to Josh and wanted to look her best for him. And as much as she pretended not to notice, she knew that he was attracted to her, too.

The kiss they'd shared that night was still rambling free in her thoughts. She'd tried to relegate it to the deep recesses of her mind where unimportant details were stored, but it refused to be held captive. At the most unexpected times, the memory would rise up and she'd catch herself reliving the moment his lips had touched hers. More times than she cared to admit, she'd found herself brushing her fingertip against her lips as if attempting to re-create the moment.

Shaking her head, she tasted the lemonade. Perfect. She poured it in cups with ice and set everything on a tray. At the last minute, she added mandarin oranges and Granny Smith apples, two of the girls' favorite treats, and then shouldered the back door open. Josh looked up at that moment and hurried to help her. He took the tray and set it on the patio table.

"I thought you might be getting thirsty," she said.

"I was. Thanks."

"Can we come get our drinks, Mommy?" Lily called.

"Yes. Just be careful walking around the swing set."

Violet and Lily walked with exaggerated steps around the play structure. Josh had been making good progress and the main part of the structure was nearly completed.

They sat at the table and drank their lemonade and nibbled on their fruit. Lily peppered Josh with questions that he answered with great patience, the smile never leaving his face. When he told a very corny joke, both girls giggled.

"I know a joke," Violet said.

"Oh, yeah. I want to hear it," Josh said.

"Okay." Violet set up straight and looked at Josh, her face very serious. "Do you want to go to a lollipop party?"

"Sure. I love parties."

She laughed. "You'll be the only sucker there."

Josh paused for a second and then laughed. "That is funny. I'm going to share that one with my friends."

"I learned that from Anthony at school."

"The boy who you beat in the spelling bee?"

She nodded. "Yep. He's the funniest kid in my class. He bought a book of jokes at the book fair and he tells them on the playground at recess. Sometimes he tells them in class, too, but the teacher doesn't like that and he gets in trouble."

"He should probably stick to the playground for his comedy act."

"Yep."

"And since you know his joke, you're funny, too."

Violet pondered that comment as if she hadn't given the idea much thought. Then she smiled. "I guess I am."

Watching Josh interact with her daughters made Kirby's heart smile. They missed so much by not having a father. Not that she was slotting Josh into the role. She barely knew him. He was young and might not be interested in being anyone's father. He might still have wild oats to sow. Besides, not everyone was cut out to be a stepparent. Some people only wanted to raise their own kids. Which was fine.

Talk about getting ahead of herself. Why was she even thinking about any of this? Not only was she unsure of Josh's feelings, she didn't have a handle on her own emotions. One minute she was ready to move on and open her heart up to someone else—or at least consider the possibility. The next, she was certain she would never love again. And if she was ready to love, that didn't necessarily mean that Josh was the man for her. There was so much they needed to discover and learn about each other.

Not only that, she needed to take the girls' feelings into account. Lily, of course, had fallen madly in love with Josh from the moment she met him. She was his little shadow, following him around with adoration on her young face. But there was Violet to consider. At times she seemed to warm up to Josh; at others she was cool. Cautious. Kirby understood that and respected Violet's feelings. And if she wasn't ready to include another person in their small circle…well, then they'd stay a threesome. Because one thing was sure—her daughters had to come first.

"Well, that was delicious. Just what I needed," Josh said, his deep voice breaking into her thoughts. He set his empty glass on the table. "Now back to work."

"I wish I could help," Lily said, poking out her bottom lip.

"You are helping me by staying at a safe distance away. And when I'm finished, you and your sister can be the first ones to try it out."

Kirby refilled the cups, leaving the pitcher on the table in case Josh wanted more, and then steered the girls back to their place under the tree. The weather was so nice that she longed to stretch out on the blanket and take a nap. Of course, she knew the minute she closed her eyes Lily would make a beeline over to Josh. So she leaned against the tree trunk and opened her book. It was either get lost in a romance or stare at Josh. She knew better than to do that or she'd start behaving as Lily had, wandering over just to be near him.

Josh screwed the last plastic rock onto the climbing wall and then stood back and inspected the play structure. He'd done a good job if he did say so himself. Lily and Violet obviously agreed. Their eyes were wide and they were grinning from ear to ear. Their hands were clasped against their chests, and they were practically vibrating. Lily couldn't seem to keep her feet still. He stood and stepped back, shaking each pole to make sure that it was secure in its hole. He didn't want anyone who played here to be injured. He'd already checked the chains and every screw, so he knew it was secure.

The air was electric with their excitement. To be honest, he was excited, too.

"There's only one more thing that needs doing," he said slowly.

"What's that?" Violet asked.

"I need someone to play on it, to make sure it's as much fun as it looks. If only I knew where I could find some kids." He turned around slowly as he scanned the yard, his hand shading his eyes as if looking into the distance.

"We're here," Lily exclaimed, raising her hand. "We'll play on it."

He looked down at them and smiled. "All right. Then go have fun."

Squealing with delight, the girls raced around him and charged the play set. Violet jumped on a swing and Lily climbed the ladder to the slide. Their laughter surrounded him until his heart was fuller than it had ever been. He couldn't remember a time when he'd gotten such satisfaction out of a simple job. Kirby came and stood beside him, and he automatically dropped his arm around her shoulder. When she didn't pull away, he drew her to his side.

She wrapped her arm around his waist and smiled at him. "Thank you so much for doing this. As you can see, the girls are beyond thrilled."

He smiled. "I enjoyed myself."

"Keeping your hand in carpentry?"

"Between you and me, there wasn't a lot of carpentry involved. It was more like putting a puzzle together. I really didn't need my tool belt, but I thought the girls might be impressed."

"They aren't the only ones."

"Oh, really?"

"Yeah. I'm a sucker for a man wearing a tool belt."

"I'll make sure to wear it more often."

She gave him the once-over, her eyes lingering on his chest and shoulders. Unbelievably, he felt his face getting hot. What kind of man blushed?

Kirby grabbed his hand. "Come on. I think I want to give one of those swings a try."

She laughed as she pulled him across the lush lawn and then hopped on a swing. Violet had vacated hers and she and Lily had climbed the ladder to the clubhouse and were peering out the window.

"Can you see us, Mommy?" Violet called.

"I sure can."

"Do you see us, Josh?" she asked next.

"Yep. I see you both."

A moment, later, she and Lily were standing on the elevated crow's nest and looking through the plastic telescope. The girls were going to be occupied for a while, so Josh decided to make the most of the rare private moment. He stepped in front of Kirby's swing and grabbed the chains, holding her in place. "I would like to take you on another date. How do you feel about that?"

"Are you talking about a me-and-you date, or a group date with all of us?"

"I'm talking about a two-person, grown-up date. This coming Saturday, if you're free. Don't worry about getting a babysitter. My brother Brady and his wife, Harper, have twin boys Lily's age. Harper had a baby a couple of months ago. I'm sure Lily and Violet will love little Christina. I'll ask Brady and Harper to watch the girls."

Kirby laughed. "You must not like Harper very much."

"What are you talking about? She's great. I love her."

"Then you must be trying to get on her bad side."

"Meaning?"

"We're talking five kids."

"Yeah. I know. Their three and your two."

"At one time."

"I'm missing something here."

"No woman who just had a baby is going to want to watch two extra children, even if only for a few hours. If she can find a few quiet moments to herself, she's going to want to sleep. Trust me."

"Oh."

"Don't worry. I'll ask my friend Ginny to watch them. She babysits them from time to time and they absolutely adore her. If she's not available, then we can think about asking Brady and Harper."

"Then it's a date?"

"It's a date. Where are we going?"

"I was thinking we could drive to Austin for dinner. Maybe walk around and take in a few sights."

"That sounds good, but I would prefer not to be so far away from the girls. I really haven't dated much since Will died." She sighed. "To be honest, I haven't dated at all and I'm not comfortable going to Austin yet."

"I understand." And he did. He knew how protective she was of her daughters. "How about we go to Provisions? My cousins Ashley, Megan and Nicole own it."

"That sounds good. I haven't been there in a long time."

"Great. I'll pick you up at six."

"Sounds perfect."

"And on that note, I'd better get out of here."

"Thank you so much again."

"No worries."

"Girls, Josh is leaving. Come on down so you can tell him thank-you and goodbye."

The girls scampered out of the clubhouse, slid down the slide and then ran to him. Lily didn't stop until she'd wrapped her arms around his waist. "Thank you so much for building our swings and slide."

He stooped down and picked her up. "You're very welcome."

Hugging his neck, she kissed his cheek. "I love you very much."

He sucked in a breath at her innocent declaration. Moved, he took a moment to speak. "I love you very much, too."

When he set her down, Violet approached him, stopping a few feet away from him. "Thank you."

"You're welcome. I hope you and Lily enjoy playing on it every day."

"Oh, we will. This one is much better than the one at the park."

"I'm glad you think so."

Lily and Violet raced back over to the swings, leaving Josh to try and get a grip on his emotions. Lily might as well have grabbed his heart in her hands when she'd said she loved him. And Violet? Although she hadn't claimed anything of the sort, he was moved by her heartfelt thanks. How was he supposed to carry on with his day after this?

Kirby accompanied Josh through the house. When they reached the front door, her stomach began to flutter with nerves. Would he kiss her again? She shoved the ridiculous thought out of her mind. Why would he kiss her? They hadn't been on a date. He'd simply come to her house to put together the swing set for her children. And yet, even as he worked, she'd often looked up and caught him staring at her.

As they stepped onto the porch, her heart began pounding so hard she thought he might hear it. But Josh kept walking to the stairs. He was just going to leave. Disappointment slowed her pulse. He stepped onto the top step, paused, and then turned around to face her. With him standing below her, they were practically eye to eye. Mouth to mouth. His lips turned up into a devilish grin.

He put a finger under her chin, lifting it slightly. Her lips parted and she swayed toward him. Right before her eyes closed, she noticed the spark in his. This kiss was so much different than their first kiss. That one had been tentative. Sweet. The perfect first kiss. This one was hot and confident. Sizzling. Kirby could have kissed him for hours, but they were standing on her porch in the middle of the day. Besides, her daughters might come looking for her at any moment. Although she was becoming more confident that Josh was a good man, she didn't want her daughters to see her kissing him.

Reluctant, but knowing that she needed to end the kiss, she eased back. Josh lifted his head and then leaned his forehead against hers, placing his hands on her waist. They breathed heavily, in tandem, for several seconds.

"Wow," Kirby said when she was able to speak again. Her lips were still tingling from Josh's kiss and her body was humming with desire. The man could kiss.

"You can say that again."

"I would but I'm not sure my brain is ready to think that hard again."

He laughed and then kissed her again. Hard and fast. "I'll see you tomorrow."

"I'll have your cappuccino waiting for you."

Kirby watched as he sauntered down the stairs, not moving until he jumped into his truck and pulled off. Then she breathed deeply and returned to the backyard and her girls.

She couldn't wait for tomorrow to come.

Chapter Nine

"I can't believe I agreed to go to dinner with him," Kirby said to her friend Ginny on Saturday night. "What was I thinking?"

"That he's a nice man, a handsome man at that, and you want to get to know him better," Ginny said from the chair in Kirby's bedroom where she was lounging comfortably. "There's nothing wrong with that."

"But..." Kirby's voice faded as she picked up a modest blue dress and held it against her body and turned so Ginny could look at it.

Ginny frowned and shook her head. "That looks like you're going to church."

Kirby smothered a laugh. She'd worn that dress to the church choir concert last month. Tossing it aside, she picked up another dress.

"But what?" Ginny prompted when Kirby's words faded away.

"What's the point? I'm not even sure that I want to get serious about him or anyone, to be honest. What Will and I shared was so special. It can't be duplicated, so why even try?"

"Of course it can't. Will was a wonderful man and no one will ever be able to take his place in your heart or your life. But Will is gone. And he won't be coming back. He loved you with his whole heart and he wanted you to find someone to love. I'm not saying Josh is that person who can create his own place in your heart. He might be. He might not be. But there's only one way to find out, and that's to get to know him better."

"I know you're right. I just don't want to make a mistake."

"We all make mistakes. I can't tell you if this is a mistake or not. But Josh is the first guy you've been remotely interested in. That has to count for something. And there's only one way to find out. If it turns out to be a mistake, we'll deal with it."

Kirby smiled. "You know, it wasn't that long ago that I was telling you something along those lines."

"And look how great that turned out," Ginny said,

beaming with happiness. "If you hadn't pushed me to give Draper a chance, I wouldn't be as happy as I am now."

Draper Fortune and Ginny had gotten together when he'd moved next door to her. On the outside, they might seem like opposites, but they were a perfect couple.

"And I'm happy for you."

"And that dress you gave me was simply stunning," Ginny said, rising from the chair and sorting through the dresses Kirby had piled on her bed. It didn't take more than a minute for her to reject all of them. Shaking her head and muttering that Kirby had chosen the most old-maid dresses that she owned, Ginny disappeared into Kirby's closet, emerging later with two dresses Kirby's sister had bought for her a couple of months ago. Harley had decided that Kirby's wardrobe needed an upgrade so she'd bought those daring dresses. Kirby hadn't intended to wear them but she didn't want to hurt her sister's feelings by taking them back.

Ginny held one dress in each hand, her arms outstretched. "Which one of these do you want to wear?"

Kirby looked from the flaming red dress with the low-cut top, to the daring white strapless dress. The red dress fit at the waist and ended at midthigh. The white dress hugged each of her curves, but it stopped at her knees. Each was designed to turn a man's head.

"I don't think either of them is right for a first date."

"Are you kidding me? Why not?"

"Because. They have a little too much va-va-voom, if you know what I mean."

Ginny laughed. "You can never have too much va-va-voom."

"Maybe not. But it is a little early in our…well, whatever it is for such a sexy dress."

"I disagree. Remember, you never get a second chance to make a first impression and all that."

"This isn't exactly a first impression. We've been hanging around each other for a while. Plus we've gone out to dinner before."

"With the girls. So that doesn't count."

Kirby looked at the pile of dresses on her bed. Ginny moved around her, blocking the bed. "One of these. None of those."

Kirby sighed and then looked at the two dresses. "Which do you like best?"

"They're both great, but I think the red is better for dinner. The white is more like a night dancing or going to see a play or a concert."

"Really? Why?"

Ginny giggled. "This is your first official date. You might be nervous and your hand could shake.

The red dress would definitely hide spills better. Not that you're going to spill anything."

Kirby laughed and dropped onto the bed. "You're wrong for that."

"And yet I'm right."

Violet and Lily came into the room. "What's so funny?" Violet asked.

"Ginny told me a joke."

"I know a joke," Violet said.

"And I can't wait to hear it," Ginny said. "Maybe you can tell me when we're playing on the swings."

"Can we go out now, Mommy?" Lily asked.

"Yes. But be careful."

"We will."

The girls rushed from the room, their footsteps growing faint as they got farther away. After a few moments, the back screen door slammed shut. Their laughter floated through Kirby's open bedroom window.

"They love that play set," Kirby said. "And I have to admit, having it has made my life easier."

"Another point in Josh's favor," Ginny remarked.

"You sound like you're his agent."

"I just want you to give him a chance. But back to the subject at hand. Red or white?"

"You made such a convincing argument about the red that I can't say no." Kirby grabbed the white dress as well as the other rejected clothes and hung them back in her closet. She grabbed a pair of red shoes and a matching bag. "I suppose you want me to wear makeup."

"With your perfect complexion, you don't need makeup and you know it. But if you want to really dazzle him, a little blush and eyeshadow might be in order."

"I was just going to brush on a little mascara and call it a day, but I guess I'll do a little bit more."

"It couldn't hurt."

"You really are sneaky, you know that?"

Ginny laughed. "It's my superpower."

Kirby reached out and hugged her. "And I appreciate it."

"I'll go check on the girls while you get dressed. Besides, Josh will be here soon and you don't want to keep him waiting."

"Thanks so much for sitting with the girls tonight."

"They're my favorite little girls in the world," Ginny replied as she left the room, closing the door behind her.

When she was alone, Kirby took off her robe, cut the tags off the dress and then pulled it on. Ginny might have been a bit cheeky when she'd said that Kirby didn't want to keep Josh waiting, but she'd been right. Not because she was anxious to see him. Okay, she might be a little bit anxious, who was she kidding? But because she always did her best to respect other people and their time. Deliberately keeping someone waiting was rude.

She sat at her makeup table and carefully applied blush, eyeshadow and mascara. It felt strange to be getting dressed for a date with a man other than Will, but she knew he'd understand. As she brushed on her lipstick, she reflected on the promises Will had extracted from her when he was lying on his deathbed. It had been easy to keep the vow she'd made to continue to run the coffee shop. It had been her dream.

She was still struggling with the other assurance she'd given him—that she'd find love again. Will had made her swear that when a good man came her way, she'd give him a chance to win her heart. At the time, Kirby had wanted to bury her heart in the grave with Will, but he wouldn't hear of it. He'd loved her too much to want her to be alone for the rest of her life. *If you won't do it for yourself, do it for me. Do it for the girls.* It had been hard to give him her word, but she'd sworn that if the right man came along she wouldn't send him away without giving him a chance to prove himself. Which was why she was going on this date with Josh even though the very thought of letting him get close to her heart scared her witless.

Kirby finished with her hair and makeup, spritzed on perfume and checked her appearance in the mirror. Ginny was right. The dress was perfect. If she was going to give Josh a chance, she might as well do it looking her best.

The doorbell rang and she gathered her purse and a wrap. "Well," she told her reflection, "here goes nothing."

As she was making her way downstairs, her daughters raced past her to the front door, Ginny right behind them. "We were inside getting a drink when the doorbell rang."

"It's Josh," Lily called. "Can we let him in?"

"I suppose so," Kirby said.

Ginny grabbed her arm before she could step away. "You look fabulous."

"You think so?"

"Yeah. Like I think I should call 911 in case he has a heart attack when he sees you."

Kirby laughed. "I'm hoping for a reaction a little less lethal than that."

Ginny whipped out her phone and winked. "Just in case."

Kirby stepped into the front room, her sudden nervousness making breathing difficult. Josh was standing in the middle of the room, Lily clinging to his arm and Violet talking to him. Kirby couldn't tell if Violet was telling him a joke or if she was sharing the fact that she'd won another spelling bee at school. Either way, Kirby was glad to see it. Of course, Violet's mood changed with the wind so who knew how long it would last before she went back to being cool.

For a moment, Kirby wondered if her own mixed feelings about having a relationship with Josh were influencing her daughter's behavior. That was something to consider. Another time.

"Hello, Josh," Kirby said.

"H-h-hey," he said. His eyes lit up and he smiled, then cleared his throat. "Hello."

"You look so pretty, Mommy," Violet said, leaving Josh's side and dashing over to Kirby.

"Thanks, sweetie."

"Doesn't Mommy look pretty, Josh?" Lily said.

Josh looked directly at Kirby, his eyes intense. "Your mom is absolutely beautiful."

"Thank you," Kirby said.

He looked as flustered as she felt for a minute and then reached down and picked up the bouquet he'd set on the coffee table. "This is for you."

"It's lovely."

"I wish you'd brought candy for Mommy again," Violet said. "It was really good. Almost as good as M&M's with peanuts. They're my favorite."

"Why didn't you bring us anything?" Lily asked.

Josh looked flummoxed and Kirby laughed. "We like Josh even when he doesn't bring us gifts, right, girls?"

"Yes," Violet said.

Lily nodded. “But we like him when he brings us presents, too.”

“I’ll keep that in mind,” Josh said, smothering a smile.

“I’ll put those flowers in a vase for you,” Ginny said. “You don’t want to be late for your reservation.”

“Thanks.” Kirby hugged and kissed each of her girls. “Be good for Ginny.”

“We will,” the girls chorused. “Bye.”

They dashed away followed closely by Ginny. Kirby and Josh stood alone in the front room, staring at each other.

“You really do look gorgeous,” he said.

“Thanks. And might I add that you look pretty nice yourself.” Although he looked great in his jeans and work shirts, he was off-the-charts handsome in his navy suit, white shirt and blue pattern tie. The suit jacket emphasized his muscular physique, outlining his broad shoulders and narrow waist.

He held out his arm and she took it, allowing him to escort her out the door and down the stairs. Instead of his pickup truck, there was a spotless black sedan parked in front of her house. She raised an eyebrow as he held open the front passenger door.

“I couldn’t take the prettiest girl in town to dinner in my work truck,” he said.

Her heart fluttered at his compliment as she got into the car. The black leather was soft to the touch, and she closed her eyes, inhaling deeply to regain a semblance of control. She and Josh had spent a lot of time together over the past few weeks, and for the most part she'd been relaxed. Now, though, every nerve ending in her body was on high alert, and she felt uncertain of how to act in his presence.

He took off his suit jacket and hung it on the hook behind the driver's seat before getting in and turning on the engine. "Do you want to listen to some music? I curated a special playlist for our drive to the restaurant."

"Did you, now? I can't wait to hear what's on it. You can tell a lot about a man by what he listens to in the car."

"Is that so? I've never heard that before."

"Possibly because I just made it up."

"Well, I don't know how much you're going to learn from this playlist. It's not what I listen to. I call this playlist 'music to drive by while taking Kirby to the restaurant on our first date.'"

She giggled. "All that?"

"I do like to be specific."

"Then I'd love to hear what you've selected."

Josh pressed a few buttons on his phone, syncing it to the car, then scrolled through his playlists until he hit upon the right one. A minute later a saxophone came through the speaker. Kirby listened for a few seconds, then turned to him. He was driving down the road, but she could tell by the stiff way he held his shoulders that he was waiting for her reaction. "You think I like smooth jazz?"

"I don't know. I was guessing."

"What gave you that impression?" She kept her voice emotionless. Even. "There were no smooth jazz songs on my playlist when we painted."

"Well, clearly I was wrong. Let me turn on the radio." He reached for the phone, and she put her hand on his, stopping him.

"You weren't wrong. I love Dave Koz. I've actually seen him in concert a couple of times. He puts on a great show."

"Then what was with the tone of voice?"

Kirby laughed. "I was just yanking your chain, trying to see how you would react."

He joined her laughter. "I have to tell you that you're a great actress. You had me fooled. It was a bit disconcerting, to say the least."

"You think so?"

He nodded.

"You aren't alone with feeling a bit off-kilter. I mean, you nailed my driving music so easily."

"Well, I did have help."

"What do you mean?"

"When Lily was telling me one of her stories, she let it slip that you like music without words. You play it in the car with the girls sometimes when it's your turn to choose."

"And from there you guessed smooth jazz?"

He nodded and smiled.

"Well, you have great powers of deduction. That's a point in your favor."

"One point for me," he crowed.

They listened to the music and chatted the rest of the way to the restaurant. When they arrived, he gave the hostess his name and they were immediately shown to their table. With hardwood floors, exposed brick and ductwork, and modern tables and chairs, the decor made quite a statement.

"It's really interesting to me that your cousins own two restaurants," Kirby said. "And Provisions is one of the hottest restaurants in the area right now. How great for you to have a connection so you can get reservations whenever you want."

"That is a bonus," he said, flashing a grin.

"And the Fortune money would be nice, too," she said with a laugh.

He looked at her, his expression serious. "But not all of us Fortunes have money. In fact, despite the name, my branch of the family can be considered the poor relations. My siblings and I grew up in upstate New York with very little money. For years my father didn't even know that we were related to the rich Fortunes. He still harbors some bitterness toward our wealthier relatives."

"If the money came from his family, I can understand how he might be a bit disappointed at being left out."

Josh shrugged. "Maybe. But you can't let something that happened in the past ruin your present. And I had a happy childhood. I have great brothers and a wonderful sister. My mother is the best. And although my father can be difficult at times, I love him, and I wouldn't trade him for anyone else. I like my life just fine."

He took a sip of water and then continued. "I can't imagine working at some corporate office, even if it's family-owned. I like working with my hands. There's something very satisfying about seeing the physical results of my labor. When I finish a renovation, or work on new construction, my work is there for the world to see. It will last for years. Maybe even generations. There's no better feeling than taking a rough piece of wood or partially destroyed bit of woodwork and turning it into something beautiful. I like watching a building go up and the satisfaction that comes from knowing I had a part in creating it." He paused and gave her a grin. "Or the good feeling that comes from stopping a roof from leaking."

"I totally get it. That's the way I feel about my coffee shop. The path hasn't always been easy, but it's always been worth it. Every day when I walk through the door of Kirby's Perks, I'm filled with pride. This is something that I created. I like being able to show my daughters what working hard can get them. I want them to know that they can achieve anything they set their minds to.

"But more than just being a business, Kirby's Perks is an important part of the community. We open our doors to community organizations and help whenever we can. You've already met my regulars. They're more than just customers. They're my friends."

"I really admire you. You've definitely created a place that's more than just somewhere to grab a cup of coffee and a doughnut." He set down his glass and looked at her seriously. "But you know you don't have to do it alone, right?"

"I'm not alone. I have Hillary."

"I know. But that's not what I mean. I'm sure she's a great employee, but when her shift is over, she doesn't have to worry about the roof leaking or water damage to the paint. Those are owner worries."

"True."

The waitress returned with their entrées at that moment, and the conversation stalled while their plates were set in front of them and they tasted everything.

"This is really delicious," Kirby said.

"I agree." Josh said. "But back to what we were talking about."

"The coffee shop?"

"Sort of. Don't you ever miss having someone to lean on?"

Kirby's heart nearly stopped at the question. Of course she'd missed having someone to lean on these past few years. Just because she'd managed didn't mean she hadn't come near to breaking. She was a woman, not a machine. "Of course. But there isn't anyone. Wishing won't change that fact."

Josh longed to tell Kirby that although there hadn't been anyone there for her after her husband's death, it didn't have to be that way now. He was here. He wanted to be someone she could count on. Someone she could lean on when times got hard. But from the way her face closed, he knew she didn't want to hear that. So instead, he changed the subject.

He knew he had made the right decision to talk about lighter subjects, like his childhood, when her shoulders relaxed. Every time she laughed, her eyes lit up. Thanks to his slightly exaggerated tales of growing up with five siblings, she laughed often and he grew more comfortable. It was hard to remember that this was their first official date. They had spent so much time together that he felt as if he had known her longer. Regardless of how he felt, they'd only met a few weeks ago.

And truly, there was no rush. It might be tempting to look down the road, but that wasn't fair to Kirby. Or to himself. Reading too much into a relationship and going overboard were his greatest flaws. And it hadn't worked out for him. This time he was going to do things the right way and get to know Kirby. Besides, they had her daughters to keep in mind. She didn't want them to get hurt. Neither did he.

After dinner was finished, they perused the dessert menu. "I'm totally getting the chocolate cake," Kirby said.

"It's really huge. Big enough for two."

"Not if one of the two is me. I had to share my chocolate candy with the girls. I'm going to eat the entire slice of cake all by my lonesome."

He laughed. "I'm thinking more along the lines of the fruit plate."

"You're kidding."

"What? Don't you think I need to watch my boyish figure?"

Her eyes skimmed over his shoulders and chest, her gaze leaving heat in its wake. It felt like her fingers had run over his skin. She looked back at his face and she gave him a devilish grin. "I don't think you have anything to worry about. But then, who knows what that shirt could be hiding. For all I know, you have Spanx holding your stomach in."

"There's no Spanx here," he assured her. "I'll be happy to prove it to you."

"I'll take your word for it." She sipped her wine and then winked. "This time."

He laughed and downed his water, needing to cool himself off. He was more than willing to show her what lay beneath his clothes. All she needed to do was name the time and the place.

They finished their dessert, chocolate cake for her and Chantilly cake for him. Josh paid the bill and left a generous tip, and then they went outside.

"How do you feel about a little walk?" he asked. It was still early and he wasn't ready for the evening to come to an end.

"That sounds good."

He took her hand and they started down the street. The sky was clear and the moon and stars shone brightly, illuminating their way. They didn't talk much, but he didn't feel the need to fill the silence. Just being in her company was enough for him.

After a few minutes, they turned and started back to the car. By the time they were sitting inside, listening to the playlist he'd created for the ride back to Kirby's house, he was sure that he was falling in love and there was nothing he could do about it. Too bad he didn't know if she felt the same.

Chapter Ten

Kirby looked up as the bell over the door chimed. It was Josh, coming in for his morning cappuccino. Even though she'd expected him to show up right about now, her heart skipped a beat when she saw him.

Their date three nights ago had been spectacular and she'd recounted every detail of it to Ginny when she'd gotten home. Somehow, discussing her feelings for Josh had made them more real and she'd grown nervous. She'd been tempted to retreat to a place where her heart would be safe, but Ginny's gentle encouragement had calmed Kirby's nerves and made her feel better about allowing Josh into her life. Even though Will had said it was okay for her to date again after he was gone, having a friend on her side made all the difference. Ginny had assured her that her feelings for Josh wouldn't diminish what she and Will had shared. Nothing could ever do that.

"What's good?" Josh asked and then laughed as he always did. She'd tried to get him to try other beverages, but he'd refused. *Why mess with a good thing?* he'd asked. Why indeed?

"Let me think. You look like a cappuccino kind of man, so I'm going to suggest that."

"You're the expert," he said.

She made him his cappuccino and then gave it to him along with a cruller. He'd tried a couple of muffins and a breakfast sandwich before deciding he was a cruller guy. He took a bite and smiled. "Delicious as usual."

"How's it going at work?"

"Great. No problems. And I had the opportunity to do some work on this beautiful old mansion I'm fixing up. I don't know who did the carpentry originally, but that person was a master craftsman. The detail is so intricate."

His eyes glowed with intensity as they did whenever he spoke of his work. It was nice being around someone who enjoyed his job as much as Josh did.

"Are you busy tonight?" she asked.

"Nope."

"How do you feel about having dinner at my place with me and the girls?"

"I'd love to. What time should I be there?"

"Does six work for you?"

"Yep. I'll be there with bells on."

"That I would love to see."

"It's just a figure of speech and you know it. But for you I just might find some." He wiggled his eyebrows and laughed. "Gotta go. See you later."

"Bye." Kirby watched as he walked away. He did look good in a pair of jeans.

The rest of the day flew by, and as she closed the coffee shop and then picked up her girls from school, she was filled with anticipation. When they got in the car, she relegated Josh to the back of her mind. Violet was full of stories, but Lily was somber. Quiet.

Kirby had alerted Lily's teacher to what she'd learned, but Mrs. Bennett hadn't been any more successful getting information from Lily than Kirby had been. Lily wasn't talking. Either she didn't have the words to explain her feelings, which given her age was a distinct possibility, or she was too hurt to talk. Either way, Kirby was left with that wretched helpless feeling. There had to be a way to find out what was going on with her little girl. She was just going to have to try harder to figure it out.

When they got home, the girls changed out of their

school clothes and then joined Kirby in the kitchen for their snacks.

"We're going to have company for dinner tonight," Kirby said.

"Who is it?" Violet asked as Lily kept her eyes trained on her cheese stick and grapes.

"Josh. He was so nice to put together the swing that I thought it would be nice to cook dinner for him to let him know we appreciate it." That wasn't the reason, but when Kirby saw Violet's frown when she mentioned his name, she thought it would help to remind Violet of Josh's kindness toward them.

"Oh, goody," Lily exclaimed, her eyes lighting up. "I like Josh."

"And he likes you. Both of you."

"Can I go outside and play for a while?" Violet asked.

"Sure."

"What time is he coming?" Lily asked, all smiles. Whatever was bothering her at school didn't seem to be an issue now that she knew Josh was coming over.

Kirby was glad that the cloud hanging over her daughter had vanished, but she wasn't sure she was comfortable with how attached Lily was becoming to Josh. If things didn't work out, Lily could be hurt. And then there was Violet. While she had warmed up to him and had been friendlier some of the time, there were still occasions when she seemed to resent his presence. Kirby wondered if it was Josh in particular that Violet didn't like, or if she'd be resentful of any man who showed an interest in Kirby.

"He'll be here at six," she told Lily.

"Is that soon?"

"No. But the time will pass faster if you go outside and play for a while."

"Okay." Lily ran outside and joined her sister on the swings and Kirby got busy with dinner. She'd put a roast in the slow cooker before she left for work that morning and the aroma made her mouth water. She whipped up some biscuits and boiled and mashed potatoes. At five o'clock, she called the girls in to do their homework. They grumbled for a few minutes and then settled down and completed their worksheets. When they were done, they washed up and then helped her set the table.

The doorbell rang promptly at six and Lily ran to the door, Kirby right behind her.

"I hope it's Josh," Lily said as she moved the curtain to the side and peered through the glass door. "It is!"

"Then let's let him inside. I'm sure he's hungry."

Kirby opened the door and Josh stepped inside. He'd changed out of his work clothes and was now wearing a white shirt and black jeans. "I hope I'm not too early."

"You're right on time," Kirby said.

Lily pushed past Kirby and charged Josh with outstretched arms. He stooped down and took her into his arms, giving her a big hug. "Hey, Lily. How are you?"

"I'm good."

"Glad to hear it."

He set her on her feet and then looked at Violet, who was leaning against a chair, her arms folded over her chest. Clearly, playing had not improved her mood. "Hi, Violet. How are you?"

"Hi," she replied, ignoring his question.

Lily grabbed Josh's hand. "You can sit by me, okay?"

"Okay."

"Lily, let Josh wash his hands. You and Violet can help me to put the food on the table."

"I want to show him where the bathroom is."

Kirby shook her head but Josh only smiled, clearly unbothered by the hero worship. "That would be great."

Violet and Kirby headed for the kitchen while Lily and Josh made a detour to the first-floor powder room. Lily was talking a mile a minute and her voice carried to the back of the house. Every so often Kirby heard Josh's baritone, but she couldn't quite make out his words. By the time they walked into the kitchen, Violet and Kirby had set the serving dishes on the table and filled the glasses with lemonade.

After everyone was seated, Kirby served the food and led the girls in the blessing. She was lifting her fork to her mouth when Lily began talking to Josh. She put a hand on her daughter's arm. "Let Josh eat. And you need to eat your food before it gets cold."

"Okay." She picked up a baby carrot and took a bite.

After a few minutes of silence, Lily began asking Josh all kinds of questions. "I don't mind answering," he said when Kirby would have redirected her daughter's focus once again.

Violet only spoke when spoken to. She finished eating in record time, then asked to be excused.

"Don't you want dessert? I picked up a cherry pie at the bakery."

Violet shook her head. "No. Can I go outside again?"

"I suppose so."

"I want to stay in here," Lily said, looking at Josh with love shining in her eyes.

"Then you need to finish eating," Kirby said.

"Okay."

After Lily finished eating, Kirby sent her outside to play while she and Josh straightened up.

"That was delicious," Josh said, scraping leftover mashed potatoes into a glass storage container before snapping on the plastic lid.

"Thank you." She leaned against the island and

took his hand into hers. “I want to apologize for Violet.”

“No apology is necessary.”

“She doesn’t mean to hurt your feelings.”

He nodded and they continued to clean the kitchen. They reached for a pan at the same time and their bodies brushed. Immediately the atmosphere shifted and was charged with sexual awareness. Suddenly Kirby’s body had a mind of its own and without thought, she wrapped her arms around his neck and brought his face down to hers. His blue eyes were filled with surprise, then darkened with desire.

Their lips met in a searing kiss that was much different from the ones they’d shared in the past. This kiss was hot and demanding, awakening desires that she’d shoved in a box and buried in the deep recesses of her mind. As their tongues tangled, he pulled her against him and she lost herself in his arms.

The sound of her daughters’ laughter plummeted her back down to earth and reality hit her. She was standing in her kitchen making out like a teenager while her young children were nearby. And she was fairly certain that one of her daughters wouldn’t be happy to see Kirby and Josh wrapped in each other’s arms. As a mother, she needed to consider Violet’s feelings. Especially since she, herself, wasn’t sure how involved she wanted to get with Josh.

"Whew," Josh said, panting and dragging a hand across his brow.

Despite knowing that she needed to regain control of herself, Kirby smiled, pleased to see that the kiss hadn't left Josh unaffected. "I know."

He reached for her, and though she wanted to be in his arms, she was on the precipice of losing the remaining shred of control she had. She took a step back. "We need to stop. The girls are right outside. In fact, I need to call them inside so they can take their baths and go to bed. Tomorrow is a school day."

"Okay," he said, flashing her a wicked grin. "In case you don't know it, I'm wild about you. I had a really great time and I can't wait to see you again."

She didn't know how to respond without giving away too much of her feelings. She couldn't tell him that she was starting to care a great deal for him, too. That she wished she could just let her emotions run free and see where they led her. At least not now. As much as she wanted to kiss Josh again and ignite that fire, she had two children who put a damper on the evening.

She straightened her blouse. "I'll tell the girls that you're leaving so they can say good-night."

She stepped into the yard, letting the evening air cool her overheated body as she told the girls it was time to come in. Lily slid down the slide while Violet swung high and then bailed out of her swing.

"Josh is leaving now," Kirby said as they stepped inside. "Come say goodbye. And then it's the three *b*'s for you ladies."

"What are the three *b*'s?" Josh asked.

"Bath, bed and books," Lily said. "And it's my turn to choose." She turned to Josh. "Do you really have to go home?"

"I'm afraid so. It's the three *b*'s for me, too."

Lily ran to him and gave him a big hug. "Bye. Hey, *bye* starts with *b*, so that makes four *b*'s tonight."

"Yes indeed," he agreed.

"Bye, Josh," Violet said, then turned and ran from the room.

Lily walked between Josh and Kirby to the front door, unknowingly assuring that there would be no good-night kiss. It was probably for the best, Kirby thought as she and Lily waved to Josh as he drove away.

After their baths, Kirby sat at the edge of Lily's bed and read the book the girls had agreed on. By the time she finished the story, the girls were practically asleep. She kissed each of their cheeks then went to her room. She smiled as she took her own bath and got ready for bed. That was two *b*'s. She just wished her third *b* could be a boyfriend. Sadly she'd have to settle for a book.

The next day when Josh stopped by the coffee

shop, he didn't have time to talk but he promised to call her that evening. Even though she knew it was unreasonable to be disappointed, she was. She had gotten used to her daily dose of flirting.

She was still thinking of Josh and missing the kiss that hadn't happened when she and the girls got home after school.

"Is Josh coming over for dinner again?" Lily asked as she ate her snack.

"Not today," Kirby said.

"I like when Josh eats with us," Lily said as if it had been an everyday occurrence. "He's like a real daddy."

"No, he's not!" Violet said, jumping to her feet, knocking over her glass of milk and sending her apple slices and cheese flying in the process. "And you're stupid for saying that."

"Violet, that's no way to talk to your sister," Kirby said. "Apologize right now."

"What do you care what I say?" Violet said, tears streaming down her face. "You only care about your stupid new boyfriend. You don't care about me and Lily."

"That's not true," Kirby said. She placed her hands on Violet's shoulder and attempted to hug her, but Violet pulled away.

"It is true. You don't care about me and now I

don't care about you," Violet yelled and then ran from the kitchen.

Shocked, Kirby stood listening as Violet raced up the stairs and into her bedroom, slamming the door behind her. She felt a hand grab hers and turned to see Lily, her face wet with tears. "Is Violet mad at me? Is that why she called me a bad name?"

"Oh, honey, Violet isn't mad at you." Kirby stooped down and gave her daughter a hug. Kirby was the real target of Violet's anger. "You know you aren't stupid, right?"

"I know." Lily nodded and wiped her own tears. "Why doesn't Violet like Josh?"

"I don't know."

"Well, I like him. He's my friend."

"I know."

Kirby knew she had to talk with Violet, but she decided to give her daughter a few minutes alone with her feelings. Clearly Violet wasn't ready to accept anyone new into their lives. And she had a right to her feelings. Truth be told, Violet's feelings only reinforced Kirby's doubts about getting too close to Josh. He was young and hadn't been responsible for anyone else in his life. Could she risk her children's happiness on his willingness to take on the responsibilities that children entailed? Was she being fair to any of them by expecting him to? She looked from her daughter to the spilled milk. The puddle was widening as the milk seeped across the floor. Was it an omen for her and Josh's relationship?

"Finish your snack while I clean up this mess, okay?"

Lily nodded and then climbed back into her chair. Kirby grabbed a sponge and cleaned the floor. Sighing, her heart heavy, she went to talk to Violet.

Kirby had been so concerned about Lily's problem at school that she hadn't paid as much attention to Violet. Oh, she'd noticed that her daughter was running hot and cold when it came to Josh, but since she'd been doing the same thing, she hadn't considered how deeply Violet's feelings went.

Kirby knocked on the door and then stepped inside. Violet was lying on her bed, her face buried in her pillow. Kirby picked up one of the dolls that Violet kept on her bed and then sat beside her and rubbed her back. Violet's sobs slowed and then eventually stopped. Kirby grabbed a tissue from the box on the nightstand between the twin beds and placed it in Violet's hand.

Sniffing, Violet brought the tissue to her face but didn't turn over to look at Kirby, so she simply sat there, waiting until her daughter was ready to talk. Finally as if realizing she wouldn't be able to outwait her mother, Violet turned over and sat up, keeping her eyes down so she wouldn't have to look at Kirby.

"I'm sorry," Kirby said.

Violet's head jerked up. Obviously she hadn't been expecting an apology. "For what?"

"For making you feel bad." She tipped Violet's face so that their eyes met and then held her gaze. "You and your sister are the most important people in the world to me. I love you both so much. But somehow I made you think that I care more about Josh than I care about you. It isn't true, you know. But now I know that I made you doubt how much you mean to me, so I'm apologizing."

"I'm sorry for calling Lily stupid," Violet said in a quivering voice. She began tearing up again.

"I know. And I know your sister will feel better when you apologize to her."

Violet nodded and scooted across the bed. "I'll tell her now."

"Before you go," Kirby said, "is there anything else you want to talk about? Like about Josh and why you don't like him?"

Violet shook her head. "No."

"Okay, then. Go apologize to your sister."

"I will," Violet said. She wiped her eyes and then ran down the stairs, calling for Lily. Kirby followed more slowly. Kirby's relationship with Josh was hurting Violet. Consequently, Violet was spreading the pain around, hurting her sister in the process. Even though Kirby had been experiencing doubts about Josh and the possibility of their relationship becoming serious, her heart ached when she thought about what she had to do. Breaking things off completely. Yet given the way her daughter felt, it was the only thing she could do.

When she reached the kitchen, the girls were hugging. Lily took one of her apple slices from her saucer and handed it to Violet. Kirby smiled. All was well between her daughters. They might quarrel as siblings tended to do, but neither ever held a grudge.

She sent the girls outside to play while she cooked dinner, which they ate together a while later. Violet kept Lily laughing by telling jokes she'd learned from Anthony. Kirby tried to smile, but her heart ached too badly for her to do more than turn up the corners of her mouth. Josh might only have had dinner here with them once, but Kirby missed him tonight. Worse was knowing that he wouldn't be sharing meals with them again.

Kirby had been looking forward to talking to Josh all day. But as the time for his call grew closer, she was filled with dread as she thought of what she had to do. When her phone rang, she steeled herself before answering. She couldn't do this. She had to do this.

"I hope I'm not calling too late," Josh said. His husky voice sent shivers racing down her spine. He might not be the right man for her, and this might not be the time for her to be in a relationship, but he made her feel emotions she hadn't felt in years.

"No," she said. "I'm awake."

"How was your day?" he asked.

It would be so easy to just say anything for a while, to let his soothing voice wash over her, but it would be unfair to continue this conversation, knowing what she had to tell him. "Not so good."

"What happened?" His voice was concerned and sounded as if he was ready to spring into action.

"It's Violet."

"What's wrong? Is she hurt?"

"Not in the way you mean. She had a meltdown today." Kirby decided not to mention that Lily describing him as a daddy had been the catalyst for the blowup. There was no need to add that kind of dynamic to this conversation. But on the other hand, it might just be the thing it took to get him to see that they were moving too fast. Surely he wouldn't like the idea of being a father figure to two little girls after only a couple of dates. Kirby inhaled deeply and then blew out the breath. "She accused me of caring more about you than I do about her and Lily."

Josh didn't reply for a while. The silence between them was long and heavy. Kirby didn't speak, either, giving him the space he needed to process what she'd said. It had been hours since Violet had made the accusation and Kirby was still coming to terms with it. Finally he spoke, his voice soft. "I see. And what did you say?"

"I told her it wasn't true, of course. I assured her that she and Lily mean more to me than anyone in the world."

"I suppose she's not used to anyone else being a part of your lives."

She felt her chest tighten. He had no idea how right he was. "It's been the three of us for so long. Naturally she's threatened by someone she thinks is taking her mother's attention from her."

"I understand that."

No, he didn't, not really. He couldn't understand where this conversation was leading. So she decided to spell it out for him. She inhaled and then blurted out the words. "I think it's best if we don't—"

"Are the girls asleep?"

"Of course. It's late."

"Good. I'm coming over so we can talk."

"There's nothing more to say."

"Really? Because I think there is. I know I have a lot to say. And if you're going to say what I think you're going to say, you should look me in the eyes when you do it."

"Fine." She threw off the sheet she'd been lying under and got out of bed. She wasn't going to get any sleep tonight anyway. "I'll be on the front porch."

"I'll be there in a few minutes."

"It won't change anything," she said, but he'd already ended the call. Just as well. Truth be told, Josh was right. He deserved to have this conversation in person. Breaking up with him over the phone was only slightly less tacky than doing it in a text.

She'd placed the clothes she'd worn that day in the hamper when she'd soaked in the tub earlier, so she pulled on a fresh, striped summer dress and went downstairs to wait for Josh. When his headlights appeared through the front windows, she went outside. He climbed the stairs and she led him to the porch swing where she often sat on nights when sleep eluded her. The girls' bedroom was at the back of the house, so their voices wouldn't disturb them.

Josh and Kirby sat side by side, not touching. Or speaking. Unlike other times, the silence wasn't relaxing or comfortable. It was heavy with emotions and angry words—those they'd spoken and those yet to be said. Kirby sat there for a few minutes, waiting for Josh to have his say. Not that anything could change her mind. She had Violet's well-being to consider. But he just sat there, breathing heavily.

Finally she realized that if they were going to have this conversation, she was going to have to initiate it. Since she was the one who'd decided they had to end things, she supposed that was fair.

"I care about you," she said, "but I have to put my daughter first."

"You're a mother. I wouldn't expect you to do anything less," he said, ignoring the part where she said she cared about him. "But I think you can still put your daughters—both of them—first without throwing me out with the trash."

"I wouldn't exactly call it that."

"No. What would you call it? Because that's the way it feels." His voice trembled with emotion and she knew he was hurting. Her heart ached for him—for both of them—but she couldn't let that deter her. "That's not my intention. You have to know that."

"I think you're looking for an excuse to end things between us. Violet's feelings are just the excuse you're using."

His words struck close to home and she winced. "That's not what I'm doing."

"Yes, it is," he repeated, his chest heaving. "You've used your daughters as a barrier so often with men in the past that you don't even realize when you're doing it. It's become second nature." He paused and stared into her eyes "Remember when I asked you to dinner that first time?"

She nodded.

"You instantly said that you didn't date. And you used your daughters as an excuse, as if you had been expecting me to back off the minute you mentioned them. I can still recall how surprised you were when I told you that the girls were welcome to come with us. That we'd make it a group date."

She couldn't deny that she'd been surprised. Or

that she had expected, maybe even hoped, that he wouldn't come up with an alternative that worked for her. And it had worked. Her daughters had enjoyed themselves that night.

"And that was nice. But the fact remains that Violet is not happy with the situation right now. I can't put your happiness—or mine, for that matter—ahead of hers. No good mother would. I'm sorry you don't understand. I thought we might be able to remain friends, but it doesn't seem like it's what you want."

"Friends?" He shook his head and before his eyes averted she saw the life drain out of them. She thought she saw moisture there, but he kept his gaze on the street beyond them, so she couldn't be sure. "I don't want to give you friendship, Kirby. I wanted to give you my love. All of you." And then he simply stood up and walked away."

Kirby just sat there and watched as he stalked down the stairs and hopped into his pickup. That hadn't gone at all like she'd hoped it would. But she had to admit she wasn't surprised that Josh hadn't wanted to be friends. In his place, she might have felt the same way. But he was single and carefree. He was considerate and good-looking. She wouldn't be surprised if he found a nice, childless woman to date before long.

Unsurprisingly, that thought didn't give her the least bit of comfort.

Chapter Eleven

Josh downed the dregs of the coffee that he'd picked up in a fast-food drive-through and frowned. It tasted like hot dishwater and that was being generous. If he wanted bad coffee, he could have made it himself and saved the money. But then, even if this coffee had been delicious, it wouldn't have satisfied him because it wasn't Kirby's cappuccino. But truth be told, he hadn't just become addicted to Kirby's coffee. He'd become addicted to *her*.

These past few days had been miserable. He never imagined his heart could hurt as badly as it did now and yet keep beating. Why couldn't Kirby see that they were good together? That there was nothing wrong with her choosing to be happy with him? Why couldn't she see that together they could help Violet realize that he wasn't a threat to her?

But Kirby hadn't even been willing to listen to him. The last thing he had expected was for her to be so inflexible. The easy way she'd cut him out of her life had shocked and hurt him. And he was still hurting.

He'd driven home in a fog that night, struggling to accept that the relationship had ended before they'd had a chance to figure out what they could be to each other. At least on Kirby's part. Josh had known from the first that she was the one for him. He'd tried to convince himself to slow down and control his feelings, taking the time that he'd never done in the past, but that had been impossible. You couldn't hold back the tide. He'd fallen in love—deeply in love—with Kirby and it was painful to think they were through.

After checking his watch, he picked up the phone. He'd gotten up early and gone to a new jobsite, working until he was nearly exhausted. The other guys must have sensed that he hadn't been in the mood to talk, because they'd given him wide berth. But even though he'd worked all day and it was getting late, he didn't want to go home. It didn't make a lick of sense and he didn't understand it, but his house felt lonely now. Or perhaps he was dragging the loneliness around with him.

He dialed Kane's number. Of all of his siblings, Kane would best understand the dynamics of Josh's relationship with Kirby. His wife, Layla, had been a widowed single mom when they'd met two years earlier. Kane had actually adopted Layla's young daughter, Erin. If there was a secret to winning over a child, Kane would know what it was.

"What's up?" Kane asked, answering the phone.

The words caught in Josh's throat. He couldn't just blurt out his problems now. "Are you busy?"

"Nope. Layla and Erin are out having girl time today and I'm doing the bachelor thing. I was about to throw a steak on the grill. I can put one on for you if you want to drop by."

Although he hadn't intended to have this conversation in person, it wasn't a bad idea. And a steak did sound better than the frozen dinner Josh had intended to microwave. "Yep. I can be there in about fifteen minutes."

"See you then."

Even though nothing had changed, Josh felt his spirits picking up as he drove to Kane's house. He parked and then jogged up the stairs and rang the bell.

"Come on in," his brother yelled from inside.

Josh stepped in the house and then walked into the kitchen. Kane took two bottles of beer from the refrigerator, kept one and handed the other to Josh. "You look like you could use this."

"You have no idea," Josh said. He twisted open the top and took a long pull.

"I'm about to grab the steaks from the grill. I microwaved a couple of potatoes, so get those out for me, will you?"

Josh nodded, took two plates from the cabinet and then set the potatoes on them. Kane returned and gave each of them a steak and then added broccoli he'd steamed.

"So, what's going on?" Kane asked as they sat at the table.

"It's Kirby. Or rather, it's her oldest daughter, Violet. After I fixed her roof, Kirby and I started dating. For the most part things were going well. Then Violet told Kirby that she cared more about me than she did about her, so Kirby ended things with me." Josh realized that everything he said had come out in a jumbled mess of pain and confusion, but Kane nodded and Josh knew that he'd been able to make sense of everything.

"And you're upset."

"Yes. I just don't understand. Kirby didn't even try to work things out. She wouldn't even listen to me. She just dumped me." His voice broke on the last words and he cleared his throat. He didn't want to start crying in front of his brother.

"What don't you understand? Why Kirby ended things or why her daughter felt threatened?"

"Both. It doesn't make sense." Josh sighed and shook his head. "I fell for Kirby hard."

"As usual," Kane said, dryly. He must have seen the hurt on Josh's face because he raised his hands in front of him. "Sorry. That didn't come out right. I don't want to make light of your feelings."

"This is different than those other times. What I feel for Kirby… I never felt anything close for another woman. And believe me, I tried to slow things down. Not only because of the tendency I had in the past to fall in love fast, but because of the girls. I didn't want to do anything that would hurt either of them."

"That's admirable."

"Fat lot of good it did me." Josh realized he was moping and told himself to knock it off. "And Lily loves me."

"And Lily is…?"

"Kirby's youngest daughter. We hit it off from the beginning. And Violet seemed to like me, too. At least some of the time. She was a little hot and cold, but things weren't bad. And I think with time I would have won her over."

Kane nodded.

"How do you do it?"

"Do what?"

"Everything. I wasn't here but from what I've heard, you and Layla made it work so well. So easily."

"Every single mother is different. And each situation is different. When Layla and I met, she had a lot of unresolved feelings about her late husband. We had to work through those issues together. It might have looked easy from the outside, but trust me, it was anything but."

"But Erin accepted you so easily."

"She was two when I met Layla last year. How old are Kirby's girls?"

"Lily is five and Violet is seven."

"When did their father die?"

"Three years ago."

"So Lily was two back then. Too young to have memories of her father. But at four, Violet wasn't. She might not have many memories of her dad, but she has some. In her mind, you might be trying to take his place."

"I'm not. One person can't replace another."

"You know that. But you're a grown man. Violet's a child. She probably doesn't understand what she's feeling or why, so she certainly doesn't know how to handle her emotions."

"Great. So what am I supposed to do?"

"Give it time."

"Time." Josh couldn't keep the bitterness from his voice. He'd already tried that.

"Yes. What's your hurry? Stop trying to force things to happen on your schedule and according to your plans. Life doesn't work that way. Especially when kids are involved. If it's meant to be it will be."

"What good will time do me if Kirby has already ended things with me?"

Kane shook his head and then smiled. "She didn't end things because she didn't have feelings for you, did she?"

"No. She said it was because of Violet."

"Right. And I think that given time, Violet won't feel as threatened. She might even miss you, which would mean you and Kirby could pick up where you left off. But the only way that will happen is if you give Violet time."

Josh's frown was his only reply. He didn't want to wait any longer. He was tired of waiting. He wanted to work things out with Kirby now. But clearly he wasn't going to get what he wanted.

Kirby set the last of the plates in the dishwasher and started it. Then she ripped off a paper towel and wiped down the counter. For the second time.

"Are you finished stalling yet so we can talk about what's bothering you?" Kirby's mother, Tanya, asked.

Kirby had invited her parents and her in-laws over for dinner today. After dinner, the girls had taken their grandfathers into the yard to see their play set. Right now, they were showing just how high they could swing and how much fun the clubhouse and telescope were. The grandfathers would keep the girls outside until they were called back in.

"What makes you think something is bothering me?" Kirby asked, playing for time.

"Because we're mothers," Frances, her mother-in-law, answered. "And we know you."

Kirby had known her in-laws nearly as long as she'd known her own parents. Her mother and Will's mother had been best friends since seventh grade. Although they hadn't acted as matchmakers, they'd been thrilled when she and Will had fallen in love and gotten married.

Kirby joined the women at the table and dropped into a chair. "I don't know where to start."

"The beginning always worked for me," her mother said.

"I met a guy." She glanced at her mother-in-law, unsure of how she would react.

Frances placed a hand over hers and gave it a gentle squeeze. "It's okay, Kirby. I know how much you loved Will. You were a good wife to him. But as much as we loved him, and as hard as it is to accept, he's gone now. He loved you. I know he'd want you to be happy and live a full life. He'd want you to find love again."

"I know. And I promised him that I would."

"Then what's the problem?" Tanya asked.

"Violet thinks that I only care about him and not about her and Lily."

"Violet is a little girl. She's used to having you all to herself, so any change in that is bound to be difficult for her."

"I know. And she's really happy now that he's not around anymore."

"Oh," her mother said, and she and Frances exchanged glances.

"I ended things with him," she explained so they knew who had done the breaking up. "It was the right thing to do."

"Was it?" her mother asked.

"Yes. Lily was getting too attached to him. She said...well, one afternoon she said he was like a daddy, which really upset Violet."

"Well, he did build them that great big swing set," her mother said.

"And he did take them to get hot dogs and chips. And he gave them Barbies," Frances added.

Kirby was surprised that the grandmothers knew all the details. But she quickly figured out their source. "Sounds like you've been talking to Lily. And she didn't leave out a thing."

"No, she didn't," Frances said. "And Josh sounds

like a thoughtful man. A man Will would approve of being in his daughters' lives."

"But what do I do about Violet? I can't put my feelings ahead of hers. Neither of you would do that."

"No, we wouldn't," her mother agreed. "Nor would we make ourselves miserable just because that was the easy way."

"It's not exactly easy," Kirby confessed. "I'm not happy about breaking up with Josh."

"We can tell," her mother said.

Kirby blew out a breath. "What should I do?"

"Give Violet time. Seeing you with Josh was a shock to her system. Help her to understand her feelings. Let her know that you can give love to a lot of people and it won't ever run out. No matter who comes in your life, you'll always have love for her. With enough time and assurance, she'll accept Josh or whoever you choose to be a part of your lives."

"And that will give you and Josh time to figure out what your feelings are, too," Frances added.

Kirby knew that she did need time to figure out her feelings. It would be wrong to bring him back into her life until she sorted out everything. "I guess you're right. I just need time."

The next three days she tried to get in touch with her feelings. One thing became completely clear. She missed Josh. She missed seeing him every day when he came into the coffee shop for his daily dose of caffeine. She missed talking to him every night. It was as if something vital was absent from her life.

But even though Kirby wasn't happy with the situation right now, Violet was thrilled that Josh wasn't around and she had her mother all to herself again.

Kirby glanced over at her girls, who were playing at their favorite table near the front window. Today was a teacher institute day, so they didn't have school. She'd asked them if they'd wanted to spend time with their grandparents, but Violet immediately said they preferred "helping" her at the coffee shop. Kirby had poured them cups of chocolate milk, added a dollop of whipped cream to make it fancy, and let them each select a pastry for their impromptu tea party. They'd brought dolls from home to play with and the dolls were sitting on the table. Lily had brought the Barbie that Josh had given her. She took it everywhere with her—including the clubhouse and down the slide. It was now her favorite doll to sleep with and it had a place of honor on her bed. Violet was playing with an old favorite doll, claiming to no longer like the Barbie Josh had given her.

Kirby filled an order and then went over to the girls. "Hey, are you ready for lunch?"

"I am," Lily said.

"Me, too," Violet said. "Can we go get hot dogs and chips?"

"Not today," Kirby said. "I brought sandwiches and soup from home."

"It was fun that time Josh took us to get hot dogs, wasn't it, Violet?" Lily said.

"It was okay," Violet answered, suddenly preoccupied with her doll now that Josh had been mentioned.

"Let's go wash our hands and then I'll get lunch."

Hillary covered the shop while she and the girls ate in the small office.

"Is Josh coming over tonight?" Lily asked.

Violet froze and looked at Kirby from the corner of her eye. "Not tonight, sweetie."

"I miss him," Lily said.

"I don't," Violet said instantly. "I like that it's just us. The way it used to be before we met him."

Perhaps Violet's heart wasn't thawing. Perhaps time wasn't the answer she'd hoped it would be. Maybe that had only been wishful thinking on Kirby's part. Because even though she'd put on a brave face, she missed Josh. He might not be the man she would spend the rest of her life with, but her life was definitely happier when he was in it. But she was a mother and she needed to put her daughter's feelings first and trust that her own time would come. That worked in theory, but it didn't do much in practice to soothe her aching heart.

After they finished eating their lunch, they went back up front. The girls took a board game with them and started to play. Hillary said goodbye and left for the day. Kirby spotted Justine, one of her regular customers, sitting alone.

Kirby carried the coffeepot over to the table and topped off Justine's mug. "How's it going?"

Justine picked up her mug and took a sip. She added sugar and cream before answering. "I have no complaints."

"Do you mind if I join you?"

"Please do."

Kirby pulled out a chair and sat across from Justine. Justine's baby, Morgan, was sleeping quietly in his stroller. "He's adorable. How old is he now? Six months?"

"Seven."

"That's such a wonderful age. They're just so warm and cuddly." She touched his foot, which had come out of his sock, and then smiled. "I remember when my girls were that age. Enjoy every second of it, because it goes by too fast."

"I am enjoying it. Especially now that he sleeps most of the night."

"I can relate. I remember when my girls were younger. Getting them to sleep at the same time was a challenge. Fortunately my husband was still alive then, so I wasn't outnumbered. Doing it on my own is definitely harder." She hadn't expected to be raising two kids under five on her own, but that was what happened when Will died. "Being a single mother is hard."

"You can say that again. There are times I'm so tired I don't think I can take another step, but he's worth it. I wouldn't trade my son for all the world."

Kirby wanted to ask Justine about her son's father, but she didn't. Just from the little Justine had said, Kirby knew Morgan's father was out of the picture and she got the sense that Justine didn't want to talk about it.

A customer stepped into the shop then, and Kirby gave Justine an encouraging smile before getting up to take his order. "I'll talk to you later. Duty calls."

The rest of the day passed quickly and soon it was time to go home.

"I can't wait to go home so I can play on the swings," Lily said as she and Violet put away the board games. She grabbed her Barbie and tucked it securely under her arm.

"Me, either," Violet said.

The girls raced from Kirby's office and to the front door. They were in such a hurry that Violet forgot the backpack that she'd recently started carrying everywhere. Kirby picked it up and something clattered to the floor. *It was the doll Josh had given her.*

Kirby held the Barbie in her hand and smiled. Maybe Violet's heart wasn't as closed to Josh as she'd wanted everyone to believe. Perhaps she really did only need time. For the first time in days, Kirby felt hopeful.

Josh drove down the road on the way to check on the progress at the mansion. Although his destination was straight ahead, he turned right. The way to Kirby's Perks.

This had gone on long enough. He knew she was in a bad position, having to put Violet's feelings before her own, and he admired her for being such a good mother.

As hurt as he was, he knew Kirby must be feeling the same pain. One thing he knew without a doubt was that she cared for him and that breaking up with him had been hard for her, too.

He couldn't count the number of times that he'd picked up his phone to call her, to let her know that he still cared for her and was there if she needed him, but hadn't. The harsh words they'd spoken to each other still echoed in his mind, making him cautious to seek her out to clear the air. But a little more than a week had passed and although Kane might have meant for Josh to allow more time to pass, he couldn't.

Saying goodbye had been the last thing on his mind when he'd gone to her house that night. He'd honestly believed that if they put their heads together, they would come up with a workable solution. It hadn't taken long for him to realize that Kirby had already made up her mind to break up with him and she wouldn't be changing it. She hadn't been interested in coming up with a way for them to continue to see each other while giving Violet a chance to realize that he wasn't a threat. In retrospect, he hadn't been as understanding of the situation as he should have been. Being in love with Kirby and wanting to spend time with her was no excuse for his failure.

But he couldn't change the past. The only thing he could do now was apologize and hope that Kirby was willing to forgive him. He needed her to know that his love was real, and it wouldn't vanish no matter how much time passed. She might have broken up with him, but he wasn't going to give up on them just yet. Their relationship was worth fighting for.

When he arrived at the coffee shop, he parked and then got out of his pickup. But instead of going inside, he stood on the sidewalk and stared at the building. He had absolutely no idea how she would react to seeing him. She could be angry and treat him coolly, maybe even have Hillary take his order. Or worse, she could act as if he were just another customer—as if they hadn't dated and developed feelings for each other. That thought nearly brought him to his knees and he had to take several deep breaths to steady himself. He considered leaving and giving Kirby more time but rejected the idea. Running wouldn't solve anything. And to be honest, not knowing was wrecking him. He couldn't sleep and could barely eat. This was no way to live.

Straightening his shoulders, he pulled open the door and stepped inside. The bell announced his arrival and Kirby looked up. His heart raced and the blood began pulsing in his veins as he stared at her. How he'd missed her. She was so incredibly beautiful. Her brown eyes widened as she looked at him, and then her luscious lips smiled. In a flash she was out from behind the counter and running across the room to him. He opened his arms wide and the instant that he felt her soft breasts press against his chest, he wrapped her arms around her. Lifting her into the air, he spun her around before setting her on her feet. His vision blurred for a moment and his voice failed him. He'd never been this happy in his life.

She laughed joyously and then pulled his face down to hers and kissed him. The second their lips met his desire flared to life. His longing for her was stronger than anything he'd felt before, coming close to engulfing him. With extreme effort, he pulled away. They were standing in the middle of her place of business. Without looking, he knew her customers were staring at them. He didn't want to tarnish the professional reputation she'd worked so hard to build.

He looked into her eyes and got to the point.

"I came here to apologize. I was wrong. And I'm sorry. I shouldn't have made you feel as if you had to choose between me and Violet. I know she and Lily will always come first with you. And they should."

She pressed a finger to his lips, stopping him before he could say all that he needed to. "I want to apologize to you, too. I shouldn't have pushed you away like that. If I made you feel as if you don't matter, I'm sorry. I do care for you. A lot. I'm falling in love with you."

For the first time since Kirby had ended things with him, Josh took a pain-free breath. *She was falling in love with him.* He'd longed to hear those words for the longest time. Waiting had made them even sweeter. He kissed her briefly, softly before stepping back. "I'm already in love with you."

She sighed and then smiled.

"I don't suppose you can get away for a while?" he asked.

She looked around. The regular customers were there and two people were in line. "I'll be right back."

Not wanting to be away from her, he went with her to the counter. Kirby looked at Hillary, "I'm going to take an early lunch. I'll be back in a little while."

"Okay." Hillary looked at Josh and smiled. "Take your time."

"Thanks."

Josh made the drive to Kirby's house in record

time. As they stepped inside, his heart began to pound. They sat on her sofa and he took her hand into his. There were so many things he wanted to say to her, so many thoughts and feelings he wanted to share. But now that they were alone and free to talk, words escaped him.

Actions spoke louder than words. That truth had been drilled into him from the time he was a child. It had never rung truer than it did now. Why tell her how he felt when he could show her? He leaned over, cupped her face in his hands and kissed her. He'd intended the kiss to be soft and to communicate his love and care for her. Instead it was hot and passionate, filled with his yearning for her. When he felt her lips part beneath his and her tongue sweep inside his mouth, all thought but one fled his mind. He wanted to make love to her. Now.

Pulling back, he leaned his forehead against hers. He might be willing and ready to take their relationship to the next level, but she might not be thinking along those same lines. After all, before he'd walked into her coffee shop a few minutes ago, nearly a week had passed without a word being spoken between the two of them. There was so much that they needed to iron out.

While he was still trying to catch his breath and formulate a coherent thought, Kirby stood and tugged on his hand. "I think we should take this upstairs. What do you think?"

He could barely think and certainly couldn't speak. Though he'd temporarily lost control of his brain, his body was still cooperating. In an instant, he was on his feet and following Kirby up the stairs and into her bedroom. It wasn't especially large, but with rich brown walls and cream-colored chairs, it was warm and inviting. As he looked at the queen bed, he waited to see if feelings of insecurity would hit him. When none did, he realized that he wasn't worried about competing with the ghost of Kirby's late husband. There would only be two people in this bed.

Taking Kirby into his arms, he led her to the bed and let his body tell her what he hadn't been able to say.

Kirby looked over at Josh before wrapping the sheet around her breasts. Josh was staring at her as if trying to gauge her feelings. That made two of them. She couldn't deny that making love with Josh had felt good. It hadn't just been physical release, although that had been a part of it. Her emotions had been involved. More than anything, she wished that she could stay here with him where everything was perfect, locking the rest of the world outside her bedroom door. Sadly, the world and her responsibilities weren't going away.

"I need to get back to work, and I suppose you do, too."

His face clouded over with disappointment. She thought a bit of pain flashed in his eyes, but it was gone so fast that she couldn't be sure. "I do. But I had hoped we could talk a little bit first."

"Now really isn't a good time."

"When is a good time?"

She blew out a breath and tried to see things from his point of view. He had made no secret of the fact that he cared about her. He said he was in love with her. Did he think she was using her need to get back to work as an excuse to get away from him? If so, was he wrong? She did need time alone to think. Josh was the first man she'd been intimate with since Will's death. Heck, he was the first man she'd kissed. So, as expected, she was overrun with numerous conflicting emotions that she needed to examine. Part of her felt as if she'd betrayed Will by making love with Josh, even though she knew she hadn't. Another part of her knew that Will would be happy that she was finally moving on.

Even though she doubted Josh was experiencing any of the same feelings, he was probably still a little emotionally vulnerable.

"How about you come over for dinner tomorrow?

And in the meantime, we can talk tonight after the girls are asleep."

"Okay. That sounds like a plan." He caressed her face. "I wish we had more time, but I need to get to work, too."

She leaned over and kissed him. "I wish life wasn't intruding on us. Although Hillary told me to take my time, I don't think she meant hours. I invited you over for dinner tomorrow and not tonight because I need to let the girls know you'll be coming around again. Lily will be thrilled. She's missed you."

"I missed her, too. And Violet." He cleared his throat. "But I missed you most of all."

She kissed him again. "I missed you, too."

"And I understand your predicament. So no pressure from me."

"Thank you." It was a relief to know that he wouldn't try to push her to act before she—and Violet—were ready.

She felt a little self-conscious as she looked for her clothes, which were scattered around the room, evidence of the heated desire that had consumed her.

As if sensing her discomfort, he covered his eyes with his forearm. "I won't peek."

She laughed and jumped from the bed, no longer uneasy with the prospect of being naked in front of him. The idea was ridiculous after what they'd shared. "Look all you want."

After she grabbed her clothes, she sashayed into her bathroom, took a quick shower and then got dressed. When she stepped into her bedroom, Josh was nowhere to be seen, but he had made up the bed. She found him downstairs, staring out the front window. He turned and held out an arm for her. She went to his side and leaned against him. He kissed her cheek and then nuzzled her neck. "You smell good."

"It's honeysuckle bodywash."

"I like it." He kissed her again and she found herself getting swept away.

"We need to get going," she reminded them both. Being this close to him again was playing with fire.

He kissed her one last time and then backed away. "Lead the way."

They held hands as he drove back to the coffee shop and as he walked her to the door. "I'll talk to you later."

As she watched him drive away, she smiled, hopeful that the future would be good between them.

Chapter Twelve

"Your face is really smiley," Violet said as she and Lily helped Kirby set the kitchen table that evening. She set the glasses on the place mats and then looked at Kirby.

"Really, really smiley," Lily agreed, placing forks and spoons on the napkins.

"Is that right?" Kirby asked.

"And you were singing in the car on the way home from school," Violet pointed out. That kid didn't miss a trick.

"I hope I was on key," Kirby joked.

"You sound better than Anthony," Violet said.

"Anthony of spelling bee fame?"

Violet nodded. "He sings loud but he's not good. When we're singing in class, Ms. Robinson always tells him not so loud, but he doesn't care. He thinks it's funny." Violet paused for a minute and then laughed. "It kinda is."

After spending the afternoon with Josh, Kirby had been in the mood to cook, so she'd made Cornish hens on the rotisserie, spaghetti casserole and corn on the cob.

"I love when you make little chickens," Lily said, pulling the leg off and taking a bite.

"I'm glad," Kirby said.

While they ate, they talked about school and upcoming events.

"How many days until my birthday?" Lily asked.

"Eight."

"I can't wait. I took the invitations to school and all of my friends are coming."

"I know. Their parents called me to let me know."

"I wish Josh could come," Lily said wistfully. "Do you think I could ask him?"

Kirby paused, waiting to see if Violet would object. She didn't. Instead, she just continued to eat. "Well, I think he might be able to come."

"Really?" Lily said.

"I actually talked to Josh today," Kirby added, giving the girls the G-rated version of the afternoon's events. "I invited him to come to dinner tomorrow."

"And what did he say?" Lily asked breathlessly.

"He said yes."

Lily cheered. "I'm glad. I like Josh. I wish he would come to dinner every day."

"I know you do." Kirby was starting to wish the same thing. She turned to Violet. "How do you feel about Josh coming to dinner tomorrow?"

Violet shrugged.

"You can tell me how you feel."

"I don't know. I don't feel anything. I guess it's okay if you want him to come."

That was better than nothing. Even so, Kirby knew she and Josh needed to take things slowly, giving Violet time to see that Josh wasn't a threat to her relationship with Kirby. She didn't want Violet to believe that her feelings didn't matter.

When dinner was finished, Kirby stood. "Let's go outside and play for a while."

"What about the dishes?" Violet asked.

"I'll take care of them later. It's a nice night. Let's go enjoy it."

Lily and Violet exchanged glances and as they walked out the door, Kirby heard Violet whisper, "See? Mommy is extra smiley today."

Kirby grinned to herself. Yes, she was. And it felt good.

"How much longer until my friends get here?" Lily asked. It was the day of her party and she'd been running from the kitchen to the front window for the past ten minutes.

"Not until noon," Kirby said, pouring orange juice into cups. "We still have to eat breakfast and then you need to change into your new birthday clothes."

Kirby had taken the girls shopping for summer clothes and Lily had chosen a short set for her party.

"I can't wait."

"You're going to have to. Is your sister awake?"

"Yes. She's looking at her math flash cards."

Kirby shook her head. Apparently Anthony had gotten the highest grade on the pop quiz yesterday. That hadn't sat well with Violet. Kirby supposed there could be worse things that mattered this much to Violet.

"Tell her to come eat. Your grandparents will be here soon to help set up for the party."

"And Josh?"

"Yes, he's coming. But he won't be here until later." He'd let her know that he had to check on a couple of projects, but he would be here before noon. But Kirby didn't want to give Lily a specific time just in case a problem delayed his arrival.

"Goody. I like it when he's here."

"Me, too. Now, go get your sister. The waffles will be ready by the time you girls get down here."

After breakfast, the girls took quick baths and put on their clothes for the party. Kirby was finishing with their hair when there was a knock on the front door.

"Yoo-hoo. Any birthday girls in here?" Kirby's dad called through the screen.

"Papa, I'm here," Lily said, dashing across the floor.

A moment later, her parents stepped inside. Her father, George, was carrying two shopping bags filled with wrapped gifts and her mother carried an enormous cake. Her father set down the bags and then held out his arms. The girls instantly ran over and gave him a big hug.

"Let me take that," Kirby said, taking the cake from her mother. Although Kirby was a good baker, her cakes were nowhere near as good or as elaborate as the ones her mother made. Lily had requested a three-dimensional princess cake and her grandmother had delivered. The cake stood ten inches high. The plastic torso of a princess dressed in yellow was in the top layer and the lower layers resembled a yellow and green princess dress.

Lily clapped her hands when she saw it and then hugged her grandmother. "My cake is so pretty, Nana. Thank you."

"You're welcome, sweetie."

A moment later, her in-laws arrived, their arms laden with wrapped packages. The girls squealed in delight and hugged their other set of grandparents.

Kirby greeted Frances and William and then excused herself to put the cake in the kitchen. The crowd followed her, the girls chatting a mile a minute.

Kirby had rented a bounce house and the workers rang the doorbell.

"We'll handle that," Kirby's father said gesturing to William. "And we'll take care of the balloons, too."

Kirby had rented a helium tank, too, and once her father and William had dealt with the bounce house, they began blowing up balloons. They'd done the same for each of her girls' birthday parties in the years since Will's death, so they had it down to a science. Kirby and "the grandmas," as Violet and Lily called them, filled goody bags with treats and toys while Lily and Violet bounced between the kitchen and the backyard, excitement getting the better of them.

"I pity the parents who are going to deal with these sugared-up kids tonight," her mother said, adding a package of M&M's to a nearly filled bag.

"Better them than us," Frances said, and the two of them laughed together. Of course it was funny to them. To Kirby, who was going to be left with two of those kids long after the grandparents had gone home for the night? Not so much. But it was a special occasion.

They finished the bags just as Kirby's sister, Harley, and their brother, Joseph, arrived carrying gifts.

"Where's the birthday girl?" Harley asked.

"Out back," Kirby said and then looked at her brother. "Lindsay and the kids not coming today?"

"The boys have games." Joseph said. Kirby's two nephews were great athletes who played high school baseball as well as PONY ball.

"And a kindergarten party isn't how teenage boys want to spend their Saturday?"

He laughed. "You know it. I hope Lily won't be offended?"

"Nah. She'll be thrilled to see her uncle."

Kirby hugged her brother, who then went out to join the men. She turned to her sister. "We're finished in here. Do you want to help with lunch?"

Harley nodded. Although Kirby would be serving the kids pizza and hot dogs, she had pasta salad, a fruit tray and finger sandwiches for the adults. In addition to her family and any of the parents who chose to hang around, she had invited the coffee shop regulars. They'd watched Lily and Violet grow up over the years and were now the girls' friends, too. Hillary was running the shop on her own today, but she'd sent a present for Lily.

They quickly prepared lunch and were on their way outside when the doorbell rang.

"I'll get it," Kirby said. She smiled when she saw

Josh standing there holding a gaily wrapped box. She opened the door and then kissed him. “Hey.”

“Hey, yourself.”

“Everyone is outside.” Her nerves jangled as she thought about introducing Josh to her family. Although she knew they would welcome him with open arms, she was still nervous about taking this next step in their relationship.

“Am I late? I thought the party started at noon.”

“No. Yes.” She paused and started over. “No, you’re not late. Yes, the party starts at noon.”

“It’s only 11:45.”

“I know. My family is here, and they want to meet you. And Will’s parents, too.”

“Oh.” He stopped walking and looked at her. Although he didn’t say anything, Kirby read the tension in his eyes. “How will they react?”

“They know about you.”

“But hearing about me in theory is a lot different than seeing me in the flesh.”

She nodded. “True. But don’t worry. They’re wonderful people.” Now she needed to take her own advice.

“I’m sure you’re right. But if it takes them a while to warm up to me, that’s fine, too.”

“You really are the best.” She kissed his cheek.

“It’s about time you figured that out.”

She took his arm and then led him outside. There

was a long table under the tree for presents and Josh set his there and then Kirby led him over to the adults. The grandfathers had done a great job with the yard. The colorful balloons were in bunches on the tables and also formed an arch around a chair where Lily would sit to open her gifts. They were also scattered around the yard.

"Everyone, this is my friend Josh Fortune."

"Josh of the Whitney Houston incident?" her mother joked.

"I've recognized the error of my ways," Josh said with a grin. "And I won't ever make that mistake again."

"I'm Tanya, Kirby's mother. It's nice to meet you."

"And I'm George, Kirby's dad. Ditto on what the wife said."

Kirby held her breath and then led him to Will's parents. Her father-in-law shook his hand. "It's nice to meet you, Josh. I'm William and this is my wife, Frances. Any friend of Kirby's is a friend of ours."

"That's right," Frances added warmly.

"It's nice to meet you both," Josh said.

Kirby smiled and hugged her in-laws, brushing unshed tears from her eyes. Introducing Josh to her siblings was significantly less emotional. They chatted for a moment and then guests began to arrive. Lily shrieked with joy as her best friend from school, April, arrived. They were dressed in identical outfits, which made them each exceedingly happy. They jumped up and down and hugged each other.

"Wait ten years. If that happens then, they'll each run home in horror, declaring that their lives are ruined," Harley whispered to Kirby and they both laughed.

April's sister, Mia, was one of Violet's best friends, so she'd been invited, too, so Violet would have a friend to play with. Violet and Mia dashed over to the swings and played together.

Within minutes all of the guests were present and the games began. Her brother and Josh ran most of the games and they laughed and razzed each other. Joseph had loved Will, calling him his little brother, so seeing how warm and welcoming he was to Josh made Kirby happy.

The grandmas were in charge of the prize table, helping the winners choose their prizes and pin on their ribbons. After the games, the kids ate and then gathered around the table to sing "Happy Birthday" to Lily. All of the girls oohed and aahed at the cake when Kirby set it on the table.

After the kids sang, Lily closed her eyes, made a wish and then blew out the candles.

"What did you wish for?" Josh asked.

"I can't tell you or it won't come true," Lily said seriously.

Kirby had the sneaking suspicion that Lily wished

for Josh to stick around. If so, that was a wish she could get behind.

Kirby cut the cake while Josh scooped the ice cream. Once the kids were done, everyone gathered around to watch Lily open her gifts.

"Open mine first," April said, pointing to a big box.

"Okay," Lily said, sitting on the chair decorated with ribbons, bows and balloons.

Lily opened the box and then gasped. She pulled out a doll and held it up for everyone to see. Then, doll clasped in her hand, she ran over and hugged her best friend. "I love it so much. Thank you."

"It's just like mine. Now our dolls can play together."

There were still piles and piles of gifts left and Lily's joyous reaction was repeated with each present she opened, whether big or small.

Kirby's mother shook her head. "At this rate, she'll never open everything before the party ends."

Kirby smiled. Lily was definitely Will's child. He had been so grateful for each gift he'd ever received, acting as if he'd been given a rare precious jewel. He'd always wanted to let the giver know that he'd appreciated their thoughtfulness.

Despite Tanya's dire prediction, they reached the final gift. Lily placed it on her lap and then read the tag as she had with every other one. Then she stood up. "This isn't for me."

"It's not?" Kirby had been handing over the gifts without bothering to look at the tags.

Lily shook her head.

"Who is it for, then?"

"It's for Josh."

"For me?" Josh looked perplexed. He'd been standing by Kirby's brother taking pictures with his phone. He walked over to Lily, who handed the box to him. He glanced at Kirby and she shrugged. She had no more idea what was going on than he did.

"See," Lily said, pointing at the gift tag. "It says J-O-S-H. That spells Josh."

"So it does," he confirmed. "But it doesn't say who the gift is from."

"Open it so we can see what it is."

When he hesitated, Kirby's father stepped in. "Okay, kids, Lily has opened all of her presents. There's still time to play on the swings or in the bounce house."

The kids squealed, jumped up and ran off to play. The rest of the adults followed, leaving Josh and Kirby alone.

Josh dropped into a chair and Kirby sat beside him. He couldn't imagine what was in the box or why someone had given it to him. Could it be one of those mysterious gifts the Fortunes had been receiving? He supposed that could be possible. But how had someone delivered it to the party without being noticed? But no one had noticed an outsider at his family's Christmas party, either. Whoever was leaving the gifts was good at being stealthy.

"Don't just sit there. Open it," Kirby urged.

"Right." He opened the package. It was a travel guide to Texas. A handwritten note on the title page read, *"See Chapter Five."*

"This must be a mystery gift like the ones my siblings and cousins have been receiving."

"I was just thinking the same thing," Kirby said, her voice filled with excitement. "Turn to Chapter Five."

He flipped the pages until he reached Chapter Five, which was titled "The Geology of Texas." Kirby leaned close enough so she could read the page.

"That's odd," she said. "Does the geology of Texas mean anything to you?"

"No. If it's a clue, it's too deep for me. And when you look at all of the gifts together, they still don't make sense."

"Well, let's think about it. You have a horse statue, a picture of a rose, a baby blanket, a record and now a travel guide of Texas with an emphasis on geology. Maybe they're pieces of a puzzle, and we just have to think about how they fit together."

"It's more like we have one piece to five different puzzles and they don't have any connection to one another."

Kirby shook her head. "Given that you're all part of the same family and you've received these anonymous gifts within a short period of time, that's highly unlikely."

"But why give me a book about Texas? In fact, why give me a gift at all? I haven't lived in Rambling Rose very long." And how did any of this connect to Mariana? Or did it? He searched the book, looking for the initials *MAF*, but he didn't see any. Still, that didn't mean there wasn't a connection between these gifts and the rest. There was only one way to find out. He was going to have to talk to her. In fact, he was going to have to talk to the rest of his family. Maybe one of them would know what this gift meant. Perhaps together they could figure out the message of the gifts.

"The plot thickens," Kirby said. She rose and took his hand, pulling him from his chair. "We'll have to figure it out later. It's almost four. The parents will be arriving soon, and we still have to give out the goody bags. You don't want to miss that, do you?"

No, he didn't want to miss that. He didn't want to miss anything. Being included in Lily's party, interacting with Kirby's family and friends made it even clearer that he wanted to be part of her life. Not just for special events and the occasional dinner.

He wanted to be with her all the time, having dinner with her and the kids and helping with homework. There had to be a way to let her know that he was in it for the long haul without scaring her away. He could practically hear Kane's voice reminding him to give it and Kirby time. And he would. No matter how difficult it was.

The parents began arriving a little before four o'clock. There was some general moaning and complaining as kids made it plain that they weren't through partying yet.

"One more slide," a little boy yelled, before running over to the swing set. Josh understood how he felt. He wasn't ready for the party to end, either.

"Just one more," his father called.

"Here is his goody bag," Josh said.

"Thanks," he said, taking the bag. "I bet it's filled with sugar that's going to keep him running around for hours."

"I think the cake and ice cream he ate here have that covered," Josh said dryly.

"Yeah. Looks like I'll be stopping at the park to let him run off some steam before we go home."

Josh laughed. "Sounds like a plan."

"Which kid is yours?" the guy who introduced himself as Mike asked, crossing his arms and watching as one more slide turned into two.

Josh wanted to claim Lily and Violet, but he

wasn't in a position to do that yet. "None. Kirby and I are friends."

The father looked at him closely, as if sizing him up. He must have approved of what he saw, because he nodded. "Kirby's good people."

"That she is."

"Let's go," Mike called to his kid, who slid once more before running over. "Good talking to you."

"You, too," Josh said as Mike and his son walked away.

By four twenty, only Kirby's parents and in-laws remained. When her mother started cleaning up, Kirby stopped her. "No way. You guys have done enough already. Besides, I know you and Dad have had a standing Saturday night date for years. I don't want to get in the way of that."

"But we don't want to leave this mess for you and the girls."

"Josh is here. He'll help."

"Of course I will," he hastened to agree.

"If you're sure," Tanya said, clearly weakening.

"Positive," Kirby replied.

"In that case, we'll be leaving, too," Frances said.

As the grandparents said their goodbyes, the bounce house employees arrived and made quick work of deflating and carting it away.

Kirby handed Josh a garbage bag and as he picked up cups and napkins and gift wrap, he wondered how there could be so much trash and how it could be scattered so far over the lawn. They'd given the kids balloons to take home, but there were still dozens tied on chairs. Two boys had untied a few of the ribbons holding the balloons to the chairs and several balloons were now caught in the branches of the tree.

Setting his garbage bag down, he tested a branch. It was strong enough to hold his weight, so he pulled himself up. When Lily and Violet saw what he was doing, they ran over to the tree.

"Why are you climbing the tree?" Lily asked.

"To get the balloons down," he replied.

After a moment of watching, the girls began shouting encouragement and directions to him.

When he reached the first balloon, he pushed it from the branches. Some of the helium had seeped out and Josh batted it free. It floated slowly to the ground and Lily ran over and picked it up. The other balloons were higher in the tree, so he climbed higher.

"You're almost there," Violet called. "You can do it. Just believe in yourself."

Smiling at her words, he reached out and knocked the remaining balloons free. As the other had done, they sank slowly to the ground. Lily and Violet began clapping and cheering for him.

"You did it, Josh," Lily said, clapping and dancing in a circle.

"Good job, Josh," Violet said seriously as she clapped. "You stayed focused and you did it."

Their admiration made him feel ten feet tall and he felt like a superhero who'd rescued a damsel in distress from a villain instead of someone who'd knocked a few partially deflated balloons from a tree. He lowered himself to the ground then looked back at the tree.

"That looks like fun," Violet said.

"Can we try?" Lily asked.

"Not right now. We need to finish cleaning up and get this yard back in shipshape."

Lily and Violet looked at each other and then back at him. "Okay. What should we do first?"

"Can you untie the balloons from the chairs?" Josh asked.

"And do what with them?" Lily asked.

"We should let them go," Violet said. "They might fly all the way to the sky like rockets."

"Okay," Lily said, and they dashed over to the chairs. They worked quietly until they had untied all the ribbons. Then they looked at each other and began counting down from ten. When they reached one, they yelled, "Blastoff!" and let go of the ribbons. Josh joined them as they watched the balloons float away, carried by a breeze. They sailed over the treetop and got high in the sky. The girls shaded their eyes with their hands, watching until the balloons were no longer visible.

Josh wiped bits of sticky remnants of cake and ice cream from the chairs and then began folding them. He grabbed two under each arm and carried them to the storage shed. When he came back out, Kirby was toting two chairs and he jogged over and tried to take them from her.

"I'm perfectly capable of putting them away," she said, twisting away.

"I know you are. But I'm here so you don't have to." She frowned and he smiled. "Come on, the girls are watching. You're making me look bad. I'm trying to show them how strong I am."

She laughed and shook her head, but she did relinquish the chairs. Though he'd been joking, once he'd said the words, he realized that they were true. He was trying to impress the girls. Oh, not with his strength. It wouldn't take much to convince them that he was strong. Heck, they'd been impressed by him climbing a tree and knocking a few balloons to the ground. No, he was trying to show them that he was a good man who cared for them and their mother. That he was worthy to be a part of their lives. That no matter what, he would be there for them. All of them.

Working together, they had the backyard in order in an hour. Although they had eaten at the party, the girls wanted to know what was for dinner. Kirby looked beat, but he knew that she wouldn't let her kids go hungry.

"How about grilled cheese and soup?" he suggested.

"Sounds good to me," Kirby said, and the girls nodded.

"I'll make it. You ladies go sit on the couch and rest."

"You don't have to tell me twice," Kirby said. Violet followed her to the living room, but Lily insisted on helping him. With her assistance, a task that could have been completed in twenty minutes took thirty. And he wouldn't have changed a minute of it. He liked listening as Lily talked about the party, her gifts and whatever else she felt like sharing.

As they ate dinner together in the living room watching one of the girls' favorite movies, he felt more content than he had in his life.

This was where he belonged.

Chapter Thirteen

Over the next few days, Josh spent a lot of time with Kirby and the girls. Kirby would have loved it if Josh came over every evening for dinner, but she knew that they had to take it slowly for Violet's sake. After they'd gotten on so well at the birthday party, Kirby had had high hopes, and there were times she believed Violet really liked Josh. Sometimes Violet would laugh at his jokes and share those she'd learned from Anthony, or include him in her stories about her school day. But then, as if realizing she'd let down her guard and let him get close, there were days when she pulled back. Still, Kirby knew she'd come to like Josh, once she allowed herself to.

As Kirby stood with the other parents at pickup time, she saw the girls run over to her. She gave each of them a hug and led them to the car.

"You're going to be so surprised tomorrow at family day," Lily said. "Mrs. Bennett hung our work and pictures in the classroom. Plus, we have a secret project."

"I can't wait to see it," Kirby said, turning to Violet before Lily could spill the secret. "And what about you? Do you have any surprises for me to see?"

"Nope."

"Can we ask Josh to come tomorrow?" Lily asked.

"I suppose so," Kirby said.

"He can't come," Violet wasted no time to object. "It's family day and Josh isn't part of our family."

"Mrs. Bennett said it's 'family and special people day.' And Josh is special to me," Lily insisted. "Mommy, can you ask him to come?"

"We'll see. He might be busy."

"I hope he's not," Lily said.

When they got home, they ate dinner and the girls played outside for a while. Kirby sat on the deck, keeping an eye on them, but her mind strayed to tomorrow's family day. Violet had been correct that Josh wasn't a member of the family, but the school administrators had never been a stickler for that kind of detail. They'd let the children and parents decide who was a part of their family.

Kirby was reluctant to invite Josh to attend because Violet was opposed to the idea. But then she looked at Lily. Her feelings mattered, too. And she really wanted Josh to be there. Kirby had been putting Violet's feelings about Josh first. This time she was going to put Lily's feelings first. She was going to ask Josh to attend family day with them when they spoke tonight.

As expected, Josh was thrilled with the invitation and promised to meet them at the school the following evening.

"Do I need to do anything?" he asked.

"Like what?"

"I don't know. Make a speech. Say something."

Kirby kept from laughing at his enthusiasm. She had no doubt that if she told him he had to sing a song, he'd start warming up his vocal cords now. "No. It's more of an open house type of thing. All you have to do is come."

"What's the dress code?"

"Clothes."

"What?"

She did laugh then. "It's casual. Put on whatever you feel comfortable wearing."

"Okay. I'm going to shower and change after work. I'll probably wear khakis and a blue shirt."

"That sounds perfect. I look forward to seeing you."

"I'll see you tomorrow."

* * *

Kirby and the girls stood in front of the school as they waited for Josh to arrive. When he pulled into the parking lot, got out of his car and walked over to them, Lily clapped her hands and jumped for joy. Violet only sighed. When he reached them, Lily gave him a big hug. "I'm so glad you're here. Wait until you see my desk and my classroom."

"I can't wait," he replied as Lily slipped her hand into his. Kirby kissed his cheek and then took a quiet Violet by the hand, and they all walked inside the school.

"Can we go to my class first?" Lily asked.

"Sure," Kirby said.

They stepped inside the classroom and Lily pulled Josh up to the front of the classroom to meet her teacher. "This is Josh. He's our friend."

Mrs. Bennett smiled. "It's nice to meet you, Josh."

"You, too," he replied.

Kirby and the teacher smiled as Lily showed Josh her desk. "We used to have name tags so we could copy our name on our pages, but we don't need them anymore. We know how to spell our names."

"I see."

A boy and his parents came over to the desk next to Lily's. Lily stiffened and then stood straight as she tugged Josh forward. "Ian. This is Josh. See, he's just like a daddy."

"Oh." The boy looked from Lily to Josh.

"Ian always tells me how much fun he has with his daddy," Lily told Kirby. "Then he says, 'Too bad you don't have a daddy, Lily.' And then he laughs at me and sticks out his tongue."

The boy's mother was aghast. "Ian! Why would you say something like that?"

He shrugged and looked down at his shoes.

"Apologize. Now," his father demanded in a no-nonsense voice.

"Sorry for being mean, Lily," Ian said in a small, quivering voice.

"And you won't do it again," his father added.

"And I won't do it again," Ian echoed.

Lily stared at him and then turned to Kirby. "Do I have to forgive him for being mean?"

"Only if you want to," Kirby said.

"I don't want to."

"We're also sorry," Ian's father said as he and his wife took Ian's hands and led him out of the room.

Lily stood there for a few moments in silence. Then Josh shared a look with Kirby before he knelt down in front of Lily. "Do you want to show us any more of your classroom?"

Seeming to snap out of it, Lily smiled brightly, as if a weight had been lifted from her shoulders. "I want to show you my art projects and the class turtle. And the reading rug and my cubby."

"I want to see all of it," Josh said.

Lily beamed as she acted as tour guide, showing them all the wonders of the kindergarten class. Kirby's heart warmed as she watched Josh interact with her daughter. He was so engaging and charming as he asked Lily to tell him about her artwork, and was suitably impressed by the painting. Kirby was delighted by the way Josh encouraged Lily to read the information about the class pet and the class rules. And when he asked detailed questions about each of jobs the kids were allowed to perform, her heart nearly burst out of her chest. He was so good with the girls. A natural nurturer if ever there was one.

"And here is the secret," Lily said, leading them to a low shelf on the back wall. She picked up a picture frame made of craft sticks that she'd painted. Inside were two pictures of her standing in front of a large tape measure painted on the wall. The one on the left had been taken on the first day of school, the one on the right more recently. "This is to show you how much I've grown up over the past year. Mrs. Bennett says we're big girls and boys now. Ready for first grade."

"This is a great secret," Kirby said.

"We can take it home today if we want."

"I do," Kirby said, taking the framed pictures from her daughter's outstretched hand.

Once Lily had shown them everything, they stepped into the hallway. Kirby turned to Violet. "Are you ready to show us your classroom?"

Violet glanced over at Josh before looking back to Kirby.

"If you don't want me to come, I don't have to," Josh said. "I can wait here."

"You don't want to see my room or my work?" Violet sounded offended as if she'd forgotten that she hadn't wanted Josh to come in the first place.

"I would love to see everything. But I'll only come if *you* want me to come. I won't be mad and my feelings won't be hurt if you say no."

Violet pondered that for a moment and then sighed. "You can come, I guess."

Clearly confused, Josh glanced at Kirby, who shrugged. Violet was as much a mystery to her as she was to him.

"Hi, Ms. Robinson," Violet said as they stepped into the second-grade classroom. "You already know my Mommy and Lily. This is Josh."

"Nice to see you all," Ms. Robinson replied. "Enjoy looking around."

"Josh is our friend," Lily added.

"I see. Well, welcome, Josh."

"Anyway," Violet said, "my desk is by the windows."

They followed her and she pointed out the row of

plants in paper cups. “We’re growing these for science. We water them and make sure they get enough sunlight, which is why they’re by the windows.”

“What kind of plants are they?” Josh asked.

“Tomato plants. On the last day of school, we get to take them home. I’m going to plant mine in the backyard and start a garden.”

“Nice,” Josh said.

“Can I help?” Lily asked.

“Sure. You can help me dig the hole, but I get to put the plant in the ground.”

“Thanks, Violet.”

Violet nodded and then led them to the bulletin boards at the back of the room where the perfect spelling tests hung. Violet pointed to hers. “Ms. Robinson hangs up the new tests every week. Then we put the old ones in our go-home folders.”

While they admired her work, a tall, good-looking boy approached them. He nudged Violet’s shoulder with his own. She glanced at him and then smiled more brightly than Kirby had ever seen. “Hi, Anthony.”

“Hi, Violet.” He smiled and two dimples flashed in his cheeks. He pointed at a couple standing beside him. “This is my mom and dad.”

“This is my mom and Josh,” Violet said in return.

“And me,” Lily said, pushing to the front. “Don’t forget about me. Hi, Anthony.”

“Hi, Lily.”

The adults smiled and greeted each other as the kids talked to each other.

"So that's Violet," Anthony's mother whispered, leaning closer to Kirby. "I was hoping for a chance to meet her. Anthony talks about her nonstop."

"Same here," Kirby said. "One minute he's her nemesis, getting a higher grade on a math test, the next he's the funniest kid in class."

Anthony's mother laughed. "She definitely keeps him on his toes. I actually caught him studying on the weekend."

"Mom, you have to see where I sit," Violet said, pulling Kirby away from Anthony's mother, who smiled and waved.

"I can't wait until I'm in second grade so I can do all the good things you get to do," Lily said.

"You'll do good stuff in first grade, too," Violet promised. "You're going to have lots of fun. You'll see."

Lily smiled and then hugged Violet briefly.

"Well, that's all to see," Violet said, after they looked at her desk. She made sure to point out that it was clean. "Ms. Robinson made us clean them out this afternoon before school ended so they wouldn't look like a disaster area."

"Don't forget to stop by the cafeteria and get ice cream," Ms. Robinson called as they left.

"We won't," Lily and Violet said in unison.

The cafeteria was in the school basement and Lily and Violet led the way. Once they had gotten their ice cream, they headed for the tables.

"Hey, there's April and Mia and some other kids from our classes," Lily said, pointing to a table where a lot of young kids were gathered.

"Can we go and sit with them?" Violet asked.

"Go ahead," Kirby said.

She and Josh went to a nearby table, sat down and began eating their ice cream. It was cool and refreshing, the perfect ending to a perfect day.

"Thank you so much for coming," Kirby said, wiping her hands on the paper napkin before balling it up.

"I enjoyed myself immensely. Although I have to say it took all of my self-control not to yell at that boy for teasing Lily about not having a father."

"Me, too. But I was impressed by the way his parents handled it. That should be the end of that. At least I know why she was upset those times." Kirby shook her head. It had never occurred to her even once that Lily would be teased because her father died. "To be on the safe side, I plan on talking to Mrs. Bennett to let her know what's been going on."

"That sounds like a good idea."

"Still, I think having you here helped. Showing Ian that she had a father figure in her life."

"That's one more reason I'm glad I was here." He

glanced at the girls. Anthony had joined them. He said something and everyone laughed. Apparently he was as funny as Violet claimed. Josh turned back to Kirby and took her hand. "Kirby, I want you to know that I'm serious about you. I want to be here for you. For all of you. I want to be more than a father figure. I want to be the daddy the girls need.

"I know I can never take Will's place, nor would I try. But I'll love them as if they were my own little girls. One day I hope I can marry you and prove it to you and to them."

Marry?

Just the word, let alone the whole idea of marrying him—marrying anyone—made her shaky. She hadn't been thinking that far down the road. Just having a relationship had been a big leap on her part. It would take time for her to start thinking about marriage. She didn't know what to say. Luckily she didn't have to give him an answer because technically he hadn't proposed. But even so, his words—and her lack of a response—hovered in the air between them.

When she saw the hurt in his eyes at her silence, she realized that she'd fumbled the moment. Before she could formulate a reply, the girls ran over to them.

"April and Mia had to go home," Violet said. "We finished our ice cream and Lily and I are ready to go, too."

Josh jumped to his feet. "I guess we should get going."

Kirby stood more slowly. "Josh—"

He cut her off. "It's okay, Kirby. I have to check on a jobsite." But Kirby heard the tightness in his voice.

They walked from the cafeteria, Lily and Violet between them. Fortunately neither of the girls picked up on the tension. Once they were outside, Josh walked them to their car and bid them goodnight before striding to his car without a backward glance.

Everything had gone so well until now. But all the joy and excitement had been sucked out of her. This wasn't the way Kirby had intended the night to end. But intent didn't always matter.

Kirby phoned Josh after the girls were asleep. He didn't answer and she didn't leave a message. She didn't know what she would have said anyway. She had no idea how to fix the situation or if that was even possible.

Thoughts of Josh kept her awake most of the night, and she nearly overslept. If not for Lily coming in and asking if today was a school day, she might still be in bed. She'd moved at the speed of light and had managed to get the girls fed and at school as the first bell was ringing. Now, as she was working, those thought continued to assault her.

"Here you go, one black coffee," she said, handing over the cup to her customer, a man dressed in a blue suit who appeared to be in a hurry.

"Thanks." He sipped, relaxed his shoulders and smiled. "That's delicious." Then he turned on his heels and strode swiftly from the coffee shop. Things had slowed down, and she had time to check on her regulars.

Looking around, Kirby noticed that Martin wasn't in his usual place. That was odd. She checked her watch. He should be here by now.

"Have you heard from Martin? I'm surprised he's not here," she said to Justine, who was playing with her baby.

"You don't know?" Justine asked.

"Don't know what?"

"He's in the hospital."

"What? No. What happened?" Kirby asked, sinking into a chair.

"I'm not sure. I just heard from Rebecca earlier that he was in the hospital."

Kirby looked around for the other woman, hoping to get details, but she wasn't around. She'd told Kirby that she'd sent in her manuscript to her editor and was taking a few days off.

"I don't think Rebecca knows any more than that or she would have told me," Justine said. "I'd visit him, but I don't think it's a good idea with the baby."

"Of course. I'll check on him and let you know what I find out."

"I'd appreciate it. I really do care about him."

"Me, too."

Kirby explained the situation to Hillary and then headed to the hospital. Since she wasn't family, the doctors couldn't give her any information. She wondered briefly if Martin had family. For someone who enjoyed talking as much as he did, he was pretty closemouthed when it came to his personal life. Now Kirby was sorry she'd respected his privacy and she wished she had asked.

She got his room number and then walked through the maze of hallways until she found his room. She knocked on the open door and then stepped inside. He was lying in bed with his eyes shut, but when he heard her knock, he opened them slowly.

His eyes lit up and he smiled. "Come in, Kirby."

She stepped inside. "How are you? Are you feeling up for company?"

He nodded. "I would love someone to talk to."

"Okay. But let me know if you start to tire out." She sat in the chair near his bed and patted his hand.

He adjusted the head of his bed, moving it until he was in a seated position, and then scooted around until he found a comfortable position. He dabbed at his forehead. "Whew. That took a bit more out of me than expected."

"How are you doing?" Kirby asked. She didn't want to ask about his diagnosis, but she did want him to know that she cared and that she wasn't here out of obligation.

"Pretty good for an old man."

"You're not an old man."

"I'm in my eighties. What would you call it?"

"Seasoned."

He chuckled. "If you say so. But enough about me. How are Violet and Lily?"

"Wonderful. And loving the puzzles and books that you gave Lily for her birthday."

"Good to hear. And how is Josh? Things good between the two of you?"

"Oh. They're fine." She missed him and it took all of her willpower to keep her eyes from filling with tears. Martin was sick and didn't need to listen to her woes.

"Fine. That's a weasel word if I ever heard one."

Kirby sighed. "But it adequately describes things between us. Fine."

"You know, Kirby, you're a smart young lady. More than that, you're kind. The fact that you're here visiting some old man you met at your coffee shop proves that."

"You're not just some old man, Martin. You're like family to me and my girls."

He waved away her statement, unwilling to let her

change the subject. "My point is that you're not the type of person who would lead a man on when you don't return his feelings. Anyone can see that Josh is in love with you. Not the kind of love that will vanish over time. The real, deep kind of love that lasts a lifetime. If you don't feel the same, you should let him know sooner rather than later so he can get over you and move on with his life."

Kirby nodded. What Martin said was true. The image of the hurt in Josh's eyes when he mentioned marriage in the school cafeteria yesterday flashed in her mind, and her stomach churned with regret.

"But if you do love him," Martin said after giving her time to mull his words, "and I believe you do, tell him. And then get on with living. And loving. Trust me, life is too short to waste. I'm eighty-one years old, and it seems as if my life flew by in the blink of an eye. Don't let your life pass you by without sharing it with the man you love."

That said, Martin closed his eyes and drifted off to sleep. Just talking for a few short minutes had worn him out. Clearly he was sicker than he let on, and Kirby worried about him. She felt tears sting her eyes but blinked them back.

She thought of Josh and how from the very first time they'd met, he'd proved himself to be a good and caring man. And he'd proved that countless times since. He'd gone above and beyond from repairing her roof to painting her shop. He'd been kind and caring to the girls. True he'd made a misstep by taking them to Roja, but his heart had been in the right place. He'd given Lily the affection she wanted and was giving Violet the time she needed. Not only that, he'd given Kirby time. And love.

What in the world was she waiting for? She looked at Martin and whispered to him. "I'll take your advice. I'll let Josh know that I love him."

Now that she said the words, she knew they were true. She did love Josh. And she wondered why she had resisted acknowledging those feelings for so long. She realized now that her concern that he was too young to make a commitment to her and her daughters was only an excuse to protect herself. Josh had proven time and again that he was worthy of her love and that he could be a good stepfather to Violet and Lily. It was fear that was holding her back. Fear of giving her heart to someone again. Because she knew just how devastating it could be to lose that someone. The pain that accompanied that loss. Loving was a risk. Until this very moment, it was a risk she hadn't been willing to take again.

She'd loved Will with her whole heart, and she'd been destroyed when he died. But despite the pain, she wouldn't trade one second that she'd spent loving him. Life didn't come with guarantees. There was no assurance that something terrible wouldn't happen to Josh in the future. But one thing was certain. Protecting her heart wouldn't keep her from loving him. It would only prevent her from sharing a life with him, one filled with love and laughter and so much happiness.

Stepping outside Martin's room, she pulled her cell phone from her purse so she could call Josh. Before she'd pressed the button, she glanced up and saw him striding down the hallway. Dressed in the faded loose-fit jeans that she'd come to know and love and a T-shirt advertising the local hardware store, he looked like a dream. No, he looked like her future.

She loved him. And she couldn't wait to let him know.

"Josh," she called, racing toward him.

"I stopped by the coffee shop. Justine told me that you came here to see Martin. I can't imagine that being in a hospital is easy for you."

And he'd come to be by her side, supporting her however she needed. Even after she'd hurt him yesterday. Because that was the kind of man he was. The kind of man who'd shown her over and over that he loved her. The kind of man she could trust with her heart and the hearts of her children.

"It's better now that you're here." She wrapped her arms around his neck, pulling his face down to hers. Then she kissed him, putting all the love she had for him into it. When he raised his head, she saw the question in his eyes. "I love you, Josh. I was afraid to let that love grow before because I was terrified of losing you. But I'm not afraid now. I want to spend the rest of my life with you."

His lips spread into a slow smile. "Say it again so I'll know I'm not dreaming."

"I love you, Josh Fortune. With all of my heart."

"Does that mean you'll marry me?"

"Are you asking me?"

"Yes, I suppose I am. But I can do better than that." He took her hand into his and looked into her eyes. The love she saw there stole her breath. He obviously didn't care that they were in the middle of a hospital corridor, because he went down on one knee. "Kirby Harris, I love you totally and completely. I want to spend the rest of my life making you happy. Will you marry me?"

Her heart soared with joy. "Yes. Yes, I'll marry you." She reached down and pulled him up for a kiss.

He smiled and looked at her. "What changed your mind?"

"Martin." She shared a little of what the older man had told her.

"He's right," Josh said. "I owe the man a thank-you. And we should tell him the good news."

They stepped into Martin's room, but he was still sleeping, so they left.

"When do you want to tell the girls?" Josh asked

when they were standing beside her car. Although his voice was calm, Kirby knew he was anxious.

"How about tonight? Can you come over for dinner?"

"Yes."

They kissed and when his lips met hers and his arms wrapped her, Kirby wished she could stay like that for the rest of time. But she had to get back to the coffee shop.

When she arrived at Kirby's Perks, she filled Justine and Hillary in on Martin's status. Of course, since the doctors hadn't been able to share anything specific, her knowledge was limited to what she'd seen. Martin looked tired and weak. Kirby intended to visit him again. Hopefully she'd learn more.

"Thank you," Justine said as she put Morgan into his stroller and left.

"I've got to go, too," Hillary said, pulling her purse strap over her shoulder.

"See you," Kirby said and then got back to work.

For the rest of the afternoon her thoughts warred between worry and elation. She was concerned for her friend, but thrilled she'd finally found the man she wanted to spend the rest of her life with.

Now she only had to tell the girls. Especially Violet.

"Set the table for four," Kirby said that evening.

"Who's coming?" Violet asked.

"I hope it's Josh," Lily said. "I like when he eats with us."

"You guessed right," Kirby said.

The doorbell rang then, and Lily raced to the door. Kirby and Violet followed right behind her. Kirby had intended to share the news with the girls after they ate, but since they were all in the front room now, she led the girls to the couch.

"Josh and I have something to tell you," Kirby said.

"What?" Lily asked.

Josh and Kirby glanced at each other and grinned. He took her hand into his. "I asked your mother to marry me and she said yes."

"Really?" Lily asked.

"Really," Kirby answered.

Lily clapped her hands. "My wish came true. I wished it when I blew out my birthday candles."

Kirby couldn't prevent the smile that lit up her face at Lily's reaction, but she sobered as she turned to look at Violet. It was her older daughter's reaction that had her worried.

For a moment Violet said nothing. Then she started to cry and Kirby's heart broke. She loved Josh and she knew he would be patient until both of her daughters were ready to accept him into their family. Kirby had hoped it wouldn't take Josh long to win over Violet. Now those hopes were dashed.

Kirby knelt in front of her daughter and wiped away her tears and then pulled Violet into her arms. "Don't be sad. Tell me what you're feeling. It will be okay. We won't get married until you're ready. I promise."

"I'm not sad," Violet said.

She wasn't? "Then why are you crying?"

"I don't know. I didn't plan to. And I don't know how to stop. But I'm happy."

"You're happy?" Kirby asked.

Violet nodded and looked over at Josh. "You're going to marry Mommy?"

Josh nodded. "I want to."

"And we can call you Daddy?" Lily asked, her eyes wide with hope.

Josh looked over at Kirby, who nodded. "Yes. If you want to."

"And you won't leave?" Violet asked, holding her breath as she waited for him to reply.

"Never," he promised, drawing a cross on his heart.

"And you love Lily and me, too? Not just Mommy?"

"Yes," Josh said, his Adam's apple bobbing up and down. "I love you and Lily, too. I'll be the happiest man in the world if you and Lily would be my little girls."

"We will," Lily and Violet said in unison. As one, they ran to Josh and he held them in a hug. He looked up, his eyes moist, and held out a hand for Kirby. As she joined in the embrace of their new family, her eyes filled with happy tears.

Epilogue

Kirby and Josh looked around the coffee shop and smiled at each other. Once it was clear that the girls were happy that Josh and Kirby would be getting married, they'd wanted to share their good news with their friends and family. Although they planned on having an official engagement party in the near future, they were holding an impromptu celebration at Kirby's Perks that Saturday. They were giving away free cookies to every customer. Their families had stopped by to wish them well and Kirby and Josh were thrilled to see how well her family got along with the multitude of Fortunes. They'd pushed several tables together and were talking and laughing as if they'd been friends for years.

In a break in the action, Josh grabbed Kirby's hand and led her to where his siblings, their significant others, and Marianna were gathered. "Do you guys have a minute?"

Justine was playing with her baby nearby, but there were two empty chairs at her table that he grabbed so he and Kirby could sit down.

Kirby listened as Josh quickly told them about the travel book he'd received as a present.

"Wow," Mariana said. "Another gift."

"It has to be related to the other Fortune gifts," Brian said. "It makes no sense otherwise."

"I agree," Brady said.

"But I can't figure out what it's supposed to mean. Do you have any idea how it is related? I mean I can sort of understand a horse and Texas being related. And maybe even the rose. And I can see how the baby blanket and the song Mary Ann could be related to you, Marianna," Josh said, looking at the newest member of the Fortune family. "But how in the world do they all relate to each other?"

They all looked at each other, similarly perplexed.

"Did you read the chapter?" Draper asked.

"Not thoroughly. I flipped through the pages and then skimmed the chapter. I had no idea what I was supposed to be looking for."

"Do you have the book with you?" Mariana asked.

He nodded. "I had a feeling you guys would stop by today and I wanted to show it to you." He pulled it out of a bag Kirby handed him and held it up. "The note said to see Chapter Five. It's all about the geology of Texas," he explained as he opened the book. "It talks a lot about gold and silver mines."

"Hey, do you all remember that poem?" Mariana asked. She began to recite it. "'What is mine is yours. What is yours is mines. I hope you can read between the lines. Love is forever, love never dies. You'll see it too, when you look in her eyes. MAF.' The poem didn't say mine, it said *mines*. Maybe that's another clue."

"Maybe." Josh slowly turned the pages of the chapter in question, looking carefully at each page. "It's possible I missed something."

Mariana nodded. It was clear her excitement was growing.

Josh turned a few more pages, then suddenly pointed at something. "Look. I don't know how I missed it before. There's a town called Chatelaine, Texas—and it's been underlined. Can you see it? It's kind of faded. Do you know anything about it?"

Kirby, a Lone Star native, shook her head, as did the others.

"Well," Mariana said, "I think we should investigate it further."

Kirby heard a clatter and looked up to see Justine leaning over to pick up a spoon she'd dropped, an odd expression on her face. If Kirby didn't know better, she'd say Justine looked a bit jumpy. Perhaps hearing about the mystery gifts was making her uncomfortable. Kirby shook off the thought; she was just projecting. Something entirely unrelated could be bothering her.

"So when is the big date?" Rebecca asked, walking over to them.

"We haven't set a date yet," Kirby said, putting Justine's reaction behind her and focusing on the reason for the party.

"Soon," Josh said, covering Kirby's hand with his. "We can't wait to start our lives together as a family."

Kirby agreed.

And she knew they were going to live happily ever after.

* * * * *

Look for the next book in the new
Harlequin Special Edition continuity
The Fortunes of Texas:
The Wedding Gift

Finding Fortune's Secret
by New York Times *bestselling author Allison Leigh*

On sale June 2022, wherever Harlequin books and ebooks are sold.

And catch up with the previous titles in
The Fortunes of Texas: The Wedding Gift

Their New Year's Beginning
by USA TODAY *bestselling author Michelle Major*

A Soldier's Dare
by Jo McNally

Anyone But a Fortune
by USA TODAY *bestselling author Judy Duarte*

Cinderella Next Door
by Nancy Robards Thompson

Available now!

COMING NEXT MONTH FROM HARLEQUIN SPECIAL EDITION

#2911 FINDING FORTUNE'S SECRET

The Fortunes of Texas: The Wedding Gift • by Allison Leigh

Stefan Mendoza has found Justine Maloney in Texas nearly a year after their whirlwind Miami romance. Now that he's learned he's a father, he wants to "do the right thing." But for Justine, marriage without love is a deal breaker. And simmering below the surface is a family secret that could change everything for them both—forever...

#2912 BLOOM WHERE YOU'RE PLANTED

The Friendship Chronicles • by Darby Baham

Jennifer Pritchett feels increasingly left behind as her friends move on to the next steps in their lives. As she goes to therapy to figure out how to bloom in her own right, her boyfriend, Nick Carrington, finds himself being the one left behind. Can they each get what they need out of this relationship? Or will the flowers shrivel up before they do?

#2913 THE TRIPLETS' SECRET WISH

Lockharts Lost & Found • by Cathy Gillen Thacker

Emma Lockhart and Tom Reid were each other's one true love—until their dueling ambitions drove them apart. Now Emma has an opportunity that could bring the success she craves. When Tom offers his assistance in exchange for her help with his triplets, Emma can't resist the cowboy's pull on her heart. Maybe her real success lies in taking a chance on happily-ever-after...

#2914 A STARLIGHT SUMMER

Welcome to Starlight • by Michelle Major

When eight-year-old Anna Johnson asked Ella Samuelson for help in fixing up her father with a new wife, Ella only agreed because she knew the child and her father had been through the wringer. Too bad she found herself drawn to the handsome and kind single dad!

#2915 THE LITTLE MATCHMAKER

Top Dog Dude Ranch • by Catherine Mann

Working at the Top Dog Dude Ranch is ideal for contractor Micah Fuller as he learns to parent his newly adopted nephew. But school librarian Susanna Levine's insistence that young Benji needs help reading has Micah overwhelmed. Hiring Susanna as Benji's tutor seems perfect...until Benji starts matchmaking. Micah would give his nephew anything, but getting himself a wife? A feat considering Susanna is adamant about keeping their relationship strictly business.

#2916 LOVE OFF THE LEASH

Furever Yours • by Tara Taylor Quinn

When Pets for Vets volunteer pilot Greg Martin's plane goes down after transporting a dog, coordinator Wendy Alvarez is filled with guilt. She knows a service dog will help, but Greg's just too stubborn. If Wendy can get him to "foster" Jedi, she's certain his life will be forever altered. She just never expected hers to change, as well.

SPECIAL EXCERPT FROM

Mariella Jacob was one of the world's premier bridal designers. One viral PR disaster later, she's trying to get her torpedoed career back on track in small-town Magnolia, North Carolina. With a second-hand store and a new business venture helping her friends turn the Wildflower Inn into a wedding venue, Mariella is finally putting at least one mistake behind her. Until that mistake—in the glowering, handsome form of Alex Ralsten—moves to Magnolia too...

Read on for a sneak preview of Wedding Season, *the next book in* USA TODAY *bestselling author Michelle Major's Carolina Girls series!*

"You still don't belong here." Mariella crossed her arms over her chest, and Alex commanded himself not to notice her body, perfect as it was.

"That makes two of us, and yet here we are."

"I was here first," she muttered. He'd heard the argument before, but it didn't sway him.

"You're not running me off, Mariella. I needed a fresh start, and this is the place I've picked for my home."

"My plan was to leave the past behind me. You are a physical reminder of so many mistakes I've made."

"I can't say that upsets me too much," he lied. It didn't make sense, but he hated that he made her so uncomfortable. Hated even more that sometimes he'd purposely drive by

PHMMEXP0322

her shop to get a glimpse of her through the picture window. Talk about a glutton for punishment.

She let out a low growl. "You are an infuriating man. Stubborn and callous. I don't even know if you have a heart."

"Funny." He kept his voice steady even as memories flooded him, making his head pound. "That's the rationale Amber gave me for why she cheated with your fiancé. My lack of emotions pushed her into his arms. What was his excuse?"

She looked out at the street for nearly a minute, and Alex wondered if she was even going to answer. He followed her gaze to the park across the street, situated in the center of the town. There were kids at the playground and several families walking dogs on the path that circled the perimeter. Magnolia was the perfect place to raise a family.

If a person had the heart to be that kind of a man—the type who married the woman he loved and set out to be a good husband and father. Alex wasn't cut out for a family, but he liked it in the small coastal town just the same.

"I was too committed to my job," she said suddenly and so quietly he almost missed it.

"Ironic since it was your job that introduced him to Amber."

"Yeah." She made a face. "This is what I'm talking about, Alex. A past I don't want to revisit."

"Then stay away from me, Mariella," he advised. "Because I'm not going anywhere."

"Then maybe I will," she said and walked away.

Get 4 FREE REWARDS!
We'll send you 2 FREE Books plus 2 FREE Mystery Gifts.
The Charming Checklist
HEATHERLY BELL
A Rancher's Touch
ALLISON LEIGH
FREE
Value Over
$20
The Wrong Cowboy
A Cowgirl's Secret
Melinda Curtis
Both the Harlequin® Special Edition and Harlequin® Heartwarming™ series feature compelling novels filled with stories of love and strength where the bonds of friendship, family and community unite.
YES! Please send me 2 FREE novels from the Harlequin Special Edition or Harlequin Heartwarming series and my 2 FREE gifts (gifts are worth about $10 retail). After receiving them, if I don't wish to receive any more books, I can return the shipping statement marked "cancel." If I don't cancel, I will receive 6 brand-new Harlequin Special Edition books every month and be billed just $4.99 each in the U.S or $5.74 each in Canada, a savings of at least 17% off the cover price or 4 brand-new Harlequin Heartwarming Larger-Print books every month and be billed just $5.74 each in the U.S. or $6.24 each in Canada, a savings of at least 21% off the cover price. It's quite a bargain! Shipping and handling is just 50¢ per book in the U.S. and $1.25 per book in Canada.* I understand that accepting the 2 free books and gifts places me under no obligation to buy anything. I can always return a shipment and cancel at any time. The free books and gifts are mine to keep no matter what I decide.
Choose one: ☐ Harlequin Special Edition (235/335 HDN GNMP) ☐ Harlequin Heartwarming Larger-Print (161/361 HDN GNPZ)
Name (please print)
Address
Apt. #
City
State/Province
Zip/Postal Code
Email: Please check this box ☐ if you would like to receive newsletters and promotional emails from Harlequin Enterprises ULC and its affiliates. You can unsubscribe anytime.
Mail to the Harlequin Reader Service:
IN U.S.A.: P.O. Box 1341, Buffalo, NY 14240-8531
IN CANADA: P.O. Box 603, Fort Erie, Ontario L2A 5X3
Want to try 2 free books from another series? Call 1-800-873-8635 or visit www.ReaderService.com.
*Terms and prices subject to change without notice. Prices do not include sales taxes, which will be charged (if applicable) based on your state or country of residence. Canadian residents will be charged applicable taxes. Offer not valid in Quebec. This offer is limited to one order per household. Books received may not be as shown. Not valid for current subscribers to the Harlequin Special Edition or Harlequin Heartwarming series. All orders subject to approval. Credit or debit balances in a customer's account(s) may be offset by any other outstanding balance owed by or to the customer. Please allow 4 to 6 weeks for delivery. Offer available while quantities last.
Your Privacy—Your information is being collected by Harlequin Enterprises ULC, operating as Harlequin Reader Service. For a complete summary of the information we collect, how we use this information and to whom it is disclosed, please visit our privacy notice located at corporate.harlequin.com/privacy-notice. From time to time we may also exchange your personal information with reputable third parties. If you wish to opt out of this sharing of your personal information, please visit readerservice.com/consumerschoice or call 1-800-873-8635. Notice to California Residents—Under California law, you have specific rights to control and access your data. For more information on these rights and how to exercise them, visit corporate.harlequin.com/california-privacy.
HSEHW22